"I'm sorry, Annie. I didn't think the kids would take it this hard."

"They love you," she said simply. "You've always been decent and kind to them. Lord knows, they got little enough of that from their…from Charlie."

"I hate like hell that I'm putting them through this."

"They'll live. People get over all kinds of things."

Have you? He wanted to ask, but didn't. He carried a pile of plates to the sink, wishing things were different. That he didn't have to leave. That these were his dishes, that this was his kitchen.

That she was his woman.

Dear Reader,

Valentine's Day is here this month, and what better way to celebrate the spirit of romance than with six fabulous novels from Silhouette Intimate Moments? Kathleen Creighton's *The Awakening of Dr. Brown* is one of those emotional tours de force that will stay in your mind and your heart long after you've turned the last page. With talent like this, it's no wonder Kathleen has won so many awards for her writing. Join Ethan Brown and Joanna Dunn on their journey into the heart. You'll be glad you did.

A YEAR OF LOVING DANGEROUSLY continues with *Someone To Watch Over Her,* a suspenseful and sensuous Caribbean adventure by Margaret Watson. Award winner Marie Ferrarella adds another installment to her CHILDFINDERS, INC. miniseries with *A Hero in Her Eyes,* a real page-turner of a romance. Meet the second of bestselling author Ruth Langan's THE SULLIVAN SISTERS in *Loving Lizbeth*—and look forward to third sister Celeste's appearance next month. Reader favorite Rebecca Daniels is finally back with *Rain Dance,* a gripping amnesia story. And finally, check out *Renegade Father* by RaeAnne Thayne, the stirring tale of an irresistible Native American hero and a lady rancher.

All six of this month's books are guaranteed to keep you turning pages long into the night, so don't miss a single one. And be sure to come back next month for more of the best and most exciting romantic reading around—right here in Silhouette Intimate Moments.

Enjoy!

Leslie J. Wainger
Executive Senior Editor

Please address questions and book requests to:
Silhouette Reader Service
U.S.: 3010 Walden Ave., P.O. Box 1325, Buffalo, NY 14269
Canadian: P.O. Box 609, Fort Erie, Ont. L2A 5X3

Renegade Father
RAEANNE THAYNE

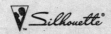

INTIMATE MOMENTS™
Published by Silhouette Books
America's Publisher of Contemporary Romance

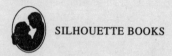 SILHOUETTE BOOKS

ISBN 0-373-27132-8

RENEGADE FATHER

Books by RaeAnne Thayne

Silhouette Intimate Moments

The Wrangler and the Runaway Mom #960
Saving Grace #995
Renegade Father #1062

RAEANNE THAYNE

lives in a crumbling old Victorian in northern Utah
with her husband and two young children. She loves
being able to write surrounded by rugged mountains and
real cowboys.

Chapter 1

Elbow-deep in blood and muck, Annie Calhoun Redhawk jerked her attention from the heifer she was helping through its first labor and stared at her foreman. Her insides suddenly felt as if the little Hereford had just shoved all four hooves hard into her gut.

"What do you mean, you're taking a job in Wyoming? You can't do that!"

Hay rustled under his boots as Joe Redhawk—her ex-husband's brother, and once her closest friend in the world—shifted his weight. He refused to meet her gaze. Instead, those hard black eyes focused on some distant point above her head in the barn rafters. "I've already done it. I just accepted Norm Waterson's offer. Told him I could start April first."

Less than two months! How could she possibly find somebody to replace Joe in just two months?

She couldn't, she realized with grim certainty, even if she had a year or more to look. He was the best cattleman in Montana—the best she'd ever known. He had unerring instincts when it came to the stock, knew just which animals to breed for the best genes, knew exactly the right feed ratios for the highest yield, knew when the weather was going to change days before it happened.

In the last eighteen months, he had singlehandedly yanked the Double C almost completely back into the black after the mess she had made of things.

"But…I don't understand. You didn't say a word about this yesterday when we went to Ennis!"

Still, he refused to meet her gaze. "I just made the decision this morning."

How would she possibly survive without him? Greasy fear churned in her stomach at just the idea. He had been more than her foreman. He had been her rock for as long as she could remember, the one safe, constant shelter in an ugly world.

"You can't leave, Joe. I—I need you." Before she could yank them back, the words she had vowed never to say to him scurried out between them like beady-eyed little barn mice.

If anything, his rough-hewn features became even more remote, his dark eyes more shuttered. "You don't need me, Annie. Not anymore. The ranch is prospering, the kids are okay. You're doing well. I told you I'd stay until you were back on your feet and I have. You're all fine now and it's time for me to move on."

As if to echo Annie's own turmoil, the heifer bawled suddenly—a high, frightened sound—and her eyes rolled back into their sockets as she strained and pushed.

"She still having a tough time?" Joe asked.

Annie turned her attention back to the animal, swallowing down the familiar feelings of betrayal and fear. Later she would have time to give in to them, but right now she had a calf to deliver.

"Yes," she answered, her voice clipped. "She's been at it most of the day but doesn't seem to be making much progress. The calf's twisted around in there pretty good. Think I'm going to have to pull it."

"Mind if I have a look?"

Without waiting for an answer, he removed the black Stetson he always wore and shrugged out of the thickly lined denim coat protecting him against the bitter weather outside. He hung both on a nail outside the stall and entered the small enclosure, rolling up the sleeves of his soft tan chamois work shirt.

As soon as he stepped inside, the bare wooden half walls seemed to close in around her. For an instant, she had a churlish urge to refuse his help. If he had his mind set on leaving, she'd have to get used to doing things on her own. Might as well start now, right?

But the heifer was in misery and needed help immediately or the calf would likely die. She couldn't let her suffer, not when Joe might be able to help. Knowing she had no choice, Annie stepped aside.

"Looks like you're right," he said after a few moments, his arm up to the shoulder inside the heifer. "I can feel the back legs right here. Let me try to turn it."

Muscles bulged under the fabric of his shirt as he worked one-handed to try maneuvering what she knew from past experience would be a slick and uncooperative calf.

"Damn. Can't do it," he muttered after several moments of trying.

The heifer bawled again, a long, pained cry, and Joe

sat back on his heels in frustration. "You have the rope?"

"Right here." She held up a length of new, clean cord purchased just for this purpose. "My hands are smaller than yours. I might have an easier time tying it."

While she tied a loop, Joe moved aside to make room. He easily held the heifer in place while Annie reached into the birth canal and worked one-handed to slip the loop around the calf's tiny hind legs.

They made a good team, she thought, not for the first time. Since he'd come to work for her, they'd had plenty of chances to work together. There was never a shortage of chores on a ranch the size of the Double C—repairing fence line, going on roundup, putting up hay. She loved every aspect of it and never missed an opportunity to help where she could.

But the rhythm the two of them developed whenever they worked together on a ranch chore went back far longer than just the last eighteen months since he'd come to work for her, back to the time she always thought of as Before.

Before that nightmare day Joe killed his father and changed the course of all their lives forever.

"Got it," she said when the rope was secured, then her hand slipped free with a loud sucking noise.

They switched places again and this time she held the heifer in place while he worked the rope. As always, he went out of his way to avoid touching her, careful to keep that discreet distance between them, like some protective barrier she could never breach.

She knew exactly why. He couldn't stand to touch her. She could tell in the way he jerked his hand away like it had been scorched if he so much as accidentally brushed her arm.

Even though she and Joe shared a friendship that went back to the days when she was little more than a carrot-headed brat in pigtails—and even though for one brief moment in time they had shared much, much more with each other—the woman she had become was weak and pitiful, frightened of her own shadow.

Joe obviously didn't like that woman any more than Annie did.

Since he'd come to the Double C she'd had plenty of time to get used to his constant subtle rejection, but it still hurt like an open wound.

Maybe it wouldn't bother her so much if she didn't crave his touch so desperately. No matter how hard she tried, she couldn't ignore this constant awareness always simmering just under her skin. She couldn't seem to control the little hitch in her breathing when he was around, or the flutter in her stomach or, of course, the memories: vivid, sun-drenched images that refused to stay buried—of fire and tenderness and skin the color of richly polished teak under her fingertips.

She closed her eyes briefly, ashamed of her weakness, that after all these years some secret part of her wouldn't let her forget.

She had made her choice and married Charlie, she reminded herself sternly. She'd had her reasons—powerful, compelling reasons. At the time marrying him had seemed like her only option. And even though her marriage had been a bitter sham, she had been faithful to the vows she'd made.

In her heart, though, she had relived those stolen hours with Joe until every second was branded into her memory.

"Almost there," he said suddenly, jolting her from her thoughts back to the straining cow. He had worked the legs free and now he let go of the rope and pulled the calf's hindquarters out. A few seconds later the little calf followed in a slick, messy heap.

The little white-faced russet Hereford lay in the hay for a few moments while his mother, acting on instincts as old as her breed, licked him clean. It wasn't long before he was stumbling to stand, eager for the colostrum so vital to his survival.

After a few shaky moments of jerking and jolting around the stall, he made it back to his mother's side, completely unfazed by the messy trauma of birth.

Annie eyed the little calf with envy. If only she had the same resilience. But she was still wobbly, teetering on legs that felt entirely too unsteady. Eighteen months wasn't nearly long enough to glue back together the pieces of her spirit Charlie had shattered.

"Good work," she said to Joe, smiling a little as the calf eagerly pulled at a teat. She watched this small miracle for a few more moments then crossed to the closest sink to scrub the muck off her hands.

Joe joined her and they lathered their hands in silence while they waited for warm water to travel from the ancient water heater at the other side of the barn. Even over the strong aroma of the soap, she could smell him—the honest scents of leather and sage and hardworking male—and her stomach did a long, slow roll.

She tested the water. Still cold. "It shouldn't be long now," she said, anxious to fill the silence that had grown suddenly awkward.

He glanced down at her, then away again. "Look, I'm sorry I didn't tell you before I was considering this job offer. But until today I wasn't sure I was even going to take it.''

At his words, the harmony created between them during the calf's delivery blew away like dry leaves in a hard October wind. She shoved her hands under the faucet, heedless of the still-icy water as all the fear rumbled back. "Why now? Why did you suddenly decide you couldn't wait to leave the Double C?''

What did I do? The thought pushed its way to the front of her mind, but she thrust it away. She was done thinking she was to blame for every single thing that went wrong in the world. Or that she could make it all better, if only she tried a little harder.

"It's time," he said quietly. "Past time." With abrupt, violent movements at odds with his low tone, he yanked a paper towel from the dispenser.

"If it's money, I can raise your salary some.''

Some, but not much, both of them knew. The blood money she had used to buy her freedom from Charlie had sapped the ranch's resources until there was very little disposable income to increase anybody's salaries.

Until the Double C had another good year or two, there wouldn't be much extra for anything.

He shook his head. "It's not about money, Annie. It's about the future. Waterson's offering me a chance to start my own herd, with an option to buy some prime land on the edge of his ranch for my own spread.''

"I...I could do the same as this Waterson's doing. Make you the same offer.''

She wouldn't beg. She was done with begging. Still, she had to try something. This was Joe. "Maybe we could work something out. I could sell you the bottom land by the river and give you part of your salary in livestock. I don't want to lose you.''

He closed his eyes briefly, as if her words hurt him. When he opened them, they were clear and determined, but with a vulnerability that shocked her. "I need to make a new start, Annie. Away from Madison Valley. Somewhere I can be just another rancher."

The soft intensity in his voice made her heart ache for him, made her ashamed of her selfishness.

Just another rancher, he'd said, not Joe Redhawk, ex-con, who couldn't walk into the grocery store in town without stares and whispers following right along behind him, even after all this time.

The rest of her arguments dwindled away into dust. He wanted to leave, to make a clean break from the shackles of his past. Even if she had the kind of power that would bind him to her, she cared about him too much to deny him his freedom.

She took a shaky breath, her stomach hollow and achy. What would the kids say when they found out he was leaving? C.J. adored his uncle and would be devastated. As to Leah's reaction, she couldn't even begin to guess. Her daughter had become a sullen stranger since Charlie left, full of lip and resentment.

At least with Joe gone, you won't have to worry so much about either of them stumbling onto the truth.

The thought whispered into her mind but was small consolation compared with the huge gaping hole his departure would leave in all of their lives.

She gnawed on her lip for a moment, then let out a breath, knowing she had no choice but to accept his decision to leave the Double C.

"Okay," she finally said. She would never be able to tell him she was happy for him at the opportunity— at least not and mean it—but she knew she couldn't argue any more.

She grabbed her coat off the rail and shrugged into it, anxious to get away from him before she did something foolish like break down. "If your mind's made up," she said, her voice only faltering a little, "I guess there's nothing more I can say. You can break the news to everyone at supper tonight and I'll start looking for a replacement."

She might be able to hire a new foreman, she thought as she walked outside to face the bitter February wind. But she knew as surely as she knew a blizzard was howling its way toward them that she would never be able to find another man to take Joe's place.

He watched her walk out of the barn, shoulders stiff and head held high, and fought the urge to pound a fist through the splintery old barn wall. He growled a curse, hating himself for putting that hurt and self-doubt back into her eyes.

She had been through so much. More than any woman should have to endure. She had finally begun to find some measure of peace in her life, finally begun to find her way again, and here he was shattering whatever serenity she had managed to create.

He had seen in her eyes how the news of his job offer had come as a crushing blow. He'd known it would, that she would see his leaving as just another in a long string of betrayals. While he hated hurting her, he didn't have a hell of a lot of choices here.

He hadn't lied about his reasons for taking Waterson's offer. He *did* want his own ranch, his own herd, his own chance to start a new life away from Madison Valley.

He just hadn't told her the whole truth.

In a furious burst of energy, he grabbed a pitchfork

and started forking fresh alfalfa into the stall for the new mama. He would never be able to tell Annie why he had to leave, why the situation here had become so intolerable to him.

He had spent four years at the state pen in Deer Lodge after his father's death—years where the only things that kept him human were the memories of Annie and his friend Colt McKendrick over at the Broken Spur and all the good times the three of them had together as kids.

As bad as his prison term was, though, it was a piece of cake compared to the self-inflicted torture of forcing himself to stay here year after year, always watching her from the edges of her life while Charlie made her life a living hell.

At first he had stayed in Ennis out of guilt and maybe some helpless, misguided effort to protect her from his brother. Then, just as he was trying to finally break away, Charlie left her high and dry on the ranch, with a mountain of unpaid bills and a ranch she had absolutely no hope of running by herself.

He leaned on the pitchfork and watched the Hereford munch the alfalfa, her calf sleeping now. He was sick to death of it. Sick of watching silently from the sidelines, sick of pining for what could never be his.

He'd been refusing Waterson's job offer for months now, ever since he met the crusty old rancher at a stock sale in Bozeman, clear back in November. Each time he talked to him, the rancher had upped the ante, but still Joe had refused, loath to put that hurt in Annie's green eyes.

But even as he continued to turn down the increasingly generous offers, he could feel his control around her slipping away faster than a Montana summer.

Except for one infamous day he preferred not to dwell on, he had kept an iron grip on himself for years. But this constant proximity to her—this playacting at being a family, with them sharing meals and decisions and work—was slowly driving him insane.

He was starting to feel like a coyote caught in one of the traps some of the ranchers set out, as if he would do anything to get away, even chew off his own leg.

The day before, he and Annie had driven into town to look at a new spreader for the tractor.

He had spent the whole damn day trying to keep his eyes on the road and not on her. Every time he caught a whiff of that apple-scented shampoo she used, he nearly drove the pickup into a tree.

And then he'd been stupid enough to take her to the diner for lunch, and the whispers had started before they'd even picked up a menu. *Murderer. Killed his father. Spent time in prison.*

He knew she heard them. Her peach-pie complexion had begun to fade, little by little, until the sprinkle of freckles that dusted the bridge of her nose stood out in stark relief.

By the time they finally made it home, he realized he would have to leave, for her sake and for his own. He just couldn't do this anymore.

He sighed heavily and put his coat and Stetson back on. He had work to do and it wasn't getting done while he stood here brooding.

The wind had picked up, he noticed as he pushed the door open and headed outside. It screeched under the eaves of the barn like an angry cat and swirled snow across the path between the house and the cluster of outbuildings and the house. The cold sneaked through his thick coat with mean, pinching fingers.

By the looks of those clouds, they'd get another foot or so tonight. A bad night to be a new calf.

The whine of brakes on the road out front sounded above the moan of the wind and he watched the school bus lumber to a stop near the house.

C.J. hopped down first, bundled up so only his eyes were showing and swinging his red backpack behind him. Leah followed more slowly, her straight dark hair—free of anything as sensible as a hat—twisting around in the wind and her hands shoved into the pockets of her coat.

No homework again, he noticed. No books, anyway. He frowned. She was never going to be able to get her grades back up to where they were before her father left if she never bothered to bring her books home from school.

C.J. spotted him first and waved wildly in greeting, then headed toward him. Leah barely acknowledged his existence with a curt nod before walking into the house. Nothing unusual there, but damned if he could figure her out. She used to always have a shy smile and a hug for him, but she'd been colder than that bitch of a wind ever since Charlie took off.

"Hey, Joe!" The boy's voice sounded distorted through his heavy scarf.

"How was school?" he asked.

He pulled the muffler down. "Good. We watched a movie about reptiles. It was awesome. Did you know there's this lizard some place in Asia that can grow to be ten feet long? Ten feet! I think it's called the Komodo dragon or somethin' like that. It can eat goats and deer and even people if they get too close."

"No, I didn't know that. Thanks for the warning. I'll keep it in mind if I ever run into one."

The boy snickered. "You won't unless you're goin' over to Asia sometime soon."

Nope. Just Wyoming. His fingers clenched inside thick gloves. "It's cold out here. You'd better go inside and get to your homework."

C.J. made a face, but turned obediently back to the house. He took a few steps, then turned back. "Hey, Uncle Joe," he said, raising his voice to be heard over the howling wind, "Nick told me a new joke on the bus today. Wanna hear it?"

He gave an inward groan. Colt's stepson told even cornier jokes than C.J. "Sure," he said. "Lay it on me."

"Knock knock."

Great. A knock-knock joke. His favorite. He winced but gave the requisite answer. "Who's there."

"Impatient cow."

"Impatient cow wh—"

"MOOOOO," C.J. cut him off before he could finish his part of the joke, then started giggling hysterically. "Get it? The cow's too impatient to wait for you to say 'who.'"

No matter how many times Annie tried to set him straight, C.J. always insisted on overexplaining his jokes. Joe smiled anyway. "I get it. That's a good one."

C.J. giggled again, then with a final wave of a mitten, he trudged through the blowing snow into the house, pausing only long enough to greet Annie's best cow dog, Dolly.

Joe watched until the boy climbed the steps to the back porch and closed the back door behind him.

He rubbed a fist over his suddenly aching heart. Damn, he would miss the little rascal. And Leah, too, even with this new frosty attitude of hers. He loved both of them as much as if they were his own kids instead of his brother's.

The future stretched out ahead of him, a bleak and solitary landscape, without Leah's smart mouth or C.J.'s corny jokes, or that soft, hesitant smile of Annie's that transformed her from an ordinary woman into someone of rare beauty.

What was he thinking to move hundreds of miles away? He would hate Wyoming without them. He should call Waterson and tell him the deal was off, that he'd changed his mind about the whole damn thing and wasn't coming after all—

He caught himself. He wouldn't do anything of the sort. He *had* to leave, and soon. If he didn't—if he gave in to the low throb of desire—Annie would run from him faster than a mule deer caught in the crosshairs.

He had already screwed up her life enough by forcing her into his brother's arms. He refused to screw it up any more.

Chapter 2

"Shut up, you little brat. It's none of your business whether I do my homework or not."

"Leah, that's enough. C.J., stay out of this. It's between me and your sister."

Annie stirred the spaghetti sauce simmering on the stove with one hand and pinched at the bridge of her nose with the other, futilely trying to squeeze out the killer headache that had formed with Joe's announcement in the barn two hours earlier and had since swollen to enormous proportions.

Thorny tendrils of pain converged behind her eyes, then snaked out in every direction throughout her head, threatening to crush the life out of any coherent thought she might have.

"Well, he *is* a little brat," Leah snapped. "I'm sick and tired of him always butting in where he doesn't belong."

"This discussion is about you, young lady. This is

the third phone call I've received from the school this month. You're seriously in danger of flunking algebra if we don't do something about it.''

''What do I care?'' Leah studied purple fingernails resting on the kitchen table, her mouth set in heavy, sullen lines. ''Mr. Sandoval's a dork.''

''He's a concerned teacher who cares enough about you and your grade to call me and inform me you're still not turning in your assignments.''

''So what?''

''So you lied to me, for starters. You told me you've been finishing all your work in study hall.''

''Algebra's stupid.''

''I like math,'' C.J. piped in.

''That's because you're stupid, too.''

''Leah, that's enough,'' Annie snapped again, feeling whatever shreds of patience she had been clinging to disappear as the headache began to writhe down her spine. ''Apologize to your brother.''

''I'm sorry you're stupid.'' Leah smirked.

With his innate sense of self-preservation, C.J. stuck his tongue out at his sister, grabbed a chocolate-chip cookie out of the boot-shaped jar on the counter, and headed for the family room.

Annie refrained from pointing out they would be eating in just a few minutes—she wasn't up to another battle, especially when his exit left her alone with the twelve-year-old daughter she barely knew anymore.

She hated this. Absolutely hated it. Leah used to be so sweet and good-natured, always eager to please, with a kind word for everyone. In the months since Charlie left she'd turned into this moody little monster with an attitude to match. She closed herself off in her room every day after school and shunned all of her mother's attempts to get to the root of the behavioral changes.

This guilt didn't help matters. Annie pinched at the bridge of her nose again.

She'd like to think this constant defiance was just a natural part of growing up, just Leah testing her boundaries as she prepared for teenagedom in a few months. But she couldn't help wondering if her daughter was reacting out of latent rage and hurt at her, if somehow she had completely warped her daughter's psyche by putting up with Charlie for so long.

She couldn't think that way. Or at least she couldn't let her guilt over her own weakness affect her treatment of her daughter.

"You're grounded." She tried not to grind her teeth at the pain in her head or at the pain in her heart. "For lying to me and for not taking care of your responsibilities. You won't be able to go to Brittany's birthday party this weekend or to any other activities with your friends until you're completely caught up in school—not just in algebra but in language arts and social studies as well.

"And," she went on, knowing this was a much worse punishment to her daughter than curtailing her social activities, "you've lost your riding privileges starting right now. Stardust is now off-limits until you manage to bring your grades up."

Leah's mouth dropped open and her eyes narrowed into a killing glare, though her lips quivered like she wanted to cry. "That completely reeks! Stardust is *my* horse. I raised her. You can't keep me from riding her!"

"Watch me." Annie turned back to add spaghetti to the now-boiling water on the stove and to hide the quiver in her own lips.

"This is *so* not fair! I hate you!" Leah cried, then stomped up the stairs to her bedroom. A few seconds later, her door slammed shut with a resounding crack that echoed through the house, making Annie flinch.

"Uh-oh. Rough day?"

She glanced toward the mudroom to find Joe's broad shoulders filling the doorway, his hands rubbing the woven band on his Stetson. She had a fierce, powerful urge to fall into his arms, to bury her face in the folds of that soft chamois shirt and weep for the daughter she didn't know how to reach anymore.

But her days of leaning were done. Joe was leaving and she would have to stand on her own two feet.

"How long have you been there?"

"Long enough to hear you ban her from that horse of hers."

"You think it's too harsh?"

He was silent for several seconds. The only sound in the kitchen was the ticking of the clock above the refrigerator and the burbling coming from the pots on the stove. "I think it's probably the only punishment that would mean a thing to her," he finally said. "She loves that horse more than just about anything."

"I had to do something. She's going to have to repeat the seventh grade if I don't."

"She doesn't really hate you. You know that, don't you?"

If she did, it would be no less than Annie deserved. For most of her daughter's life, their home hadn't been the safe haven every child deserves but a place of prolonged tension and then sharp, sudden outbursts of temper. Why shouldn't Leah hate her for the choices she'd made?

The hell of it was, if she had it all to do over again, she would probably make the same choices.

She glanced up to find Joe studying her, expecting an answer. Since she couldn't very well tell him her thoughts, she just nodded. "I know she doesn't hate me," she said, without conviction.

He looked like he wanted to pursue it, but to her relief, he changed the subject. "Have you told the kids about my new job?"

The new job. The reminder sent fresh pain slithering to the base of her skull.

She shook her head, wincing a little at the movement, while she pulled out a fragrant loaf of garlic bread from the oven. "You're the one leaving. You're the one who can break the news."

He frowned at her shortness. "Annie—"

"This is almost ready. Where's the rest of the crew?" She cut him off, not wanting to hear more apologies or explanations.

A muscle flexed in his jaw but he let the matter rest. "Patch was just about finished in the barn and I think Ruben and Manny are right behind me."

"What about Luke?"

"I think he went back to the trailer to get gussied up for you. Said something about putting on a clean shirt."

She looked up from stirring the spaghetti sauce, just in time to catch his rare grin. She gazed at it, at him.

The smile softened the harsh lines of his features, etching lines along the edges of his mouth and the corners of his eyes. He was beautiful, in a raw, elemental way with those glittering black eyes fringed by long, thick eyelashes, that sensual mouth and that coppery skin from his Shoshone heritage stretched over high cheekbones.

She blinked, suddenly breathless. "Don't tease him, Joe. He gets enough from the rest of the men."

"He wouldn't if the kid didn't make it so easy for us. He follows you around like he's a puppy dog and you're a big ol' juicy bone he wants to sink his teeth into."

"He does not." She felt her face flush from more than just the heat rising off the pans on the stove.

She was very much afraid Joe was right, that their newest ranch hand made it painfully obvious to everyone he had a crush on her. She had done her best to discourage him but he seemed oblivious to all her gentle hints. If it was causing problems between him and the rest of the help, she was going to have to be more stern.

"Does so." Joe flashed another of those rare grins. "We practically have to lift the boy's tongue off the floor every time he looks at you."

She managed—barely—to lift her own tongue off the floor and yanked her gaze away from that smile she suddenly realized she would miss so desperately.

She stirred the spaghetti sauce with vigorous motions. "He's just a little overenthusiastic. He'll get over it. Besides, don't you remember what it was like to be twenty-two?"

As soon as the words escaped her mouth, she wanted to grab them and stuff them back. The year he had turned twenty-two, she had been eighteen, and she had given him her love and her innocence on a sun-warmed stretch of meadow grass on the shores of Butterfly Lake.

Now, after her hastily spoken words, he was silent for one beat too long and she finally risked a look at him over the steam curling up from the bubbling pasta. That muscle worked in his jaw again and his dark eyes held a distant, unreadable expression.

"I do," he said softly. "Every minute of it."

Her breath caught and held, but before she could think of a reply, the outside door opened, bringing a gust of icy air, and the Santiago brothers tromped through the mudroom. The kitchen was soon filled with the sound of scraping chairs and melodious Spanish.

"That storm's gonna be a real bi…er, beast," Patch McNeil entered the kitchen behind them, his leathery cheeks red and wind-chapped above the white of the handlebar mustache he was so proud of. "I'm afraid we're gonna lose some stock tonight."

She barely heard the old cowboy, still flustered from the intense exchange with Joe. What could he have meant by those low words? Was she reading too much into it? Could he simply have been referring to being twenty-two or was he also haunted by the memory of those hours spent in each other's arms? After his release from prison, he had never given her any indication he even remembered the encounter that had forever changed the course of her life.

They had never talked about it, about the day of her father's funeral when he had come in search of her and found her lost and grief-stricken at the lake they'd spent so many hours fishing when they were younger.

While he was alive, her father had been stiff and un-affectionate, impossible to please, but she loved him desperately. He was the only parent she ever knew and his death had left her a frightened eighteen-year-old girl responsible for a six-hundred-head cattle ranch.

Joe had started out comforting her but she had wanted more from him. She had always wanted more from him.

She knew he regretted what they had done. He couldn't have made it more clear when he left Madison

Valley that night for a new job on a ranch near Great Falls, taking her heart with him.

In the years since, that hazy afternoon had become like the proverbial elephant sitting in the parlor that both of them could clearly see but neither wanted to be the first to mention.

Her mind racing, she drained the pasta with mechanical movements and spooned the sauce into a serving dish. She finally turned to set the food on the big pine table that ran the length of the kitchen and was startled to find all the men watching her, wearing odd expressions.

"What's the matter?"

"I asked twice if you wanted me to round up C.J. and Leah." Joe sent her a long, searching look and she hoped like crazy he couldn't read her thoughts on her face.

"Um, yes. Thank you."

Luke came in from outside just as Joe returned to the kitchen with C.J. riding piggyback and Leah trudging behind, resentment at her mother still simmering in her eyes.

As they began to eat, Annie thought about how much she had come to enjoy these evening meals with her makeshift family. It hadn't always been like this. During her marriage, meals had been tense, uneasy affairs that she usually couldn't wait to escape.

The first thing she had done after Charlie left was give notice to the crew he surrounded himself with, men whose insolence was matched only by their incompetence.

The second thing had been to steal Patch back from the ranch he'd gone to after she married Charlie so she could split kitchen duty with him.

In her father's day, Patch had been the camp cook. In those days, the Double C had fixed one meal a day for its hands, usually supper. The ranch provided the food for the other meals but left it up to the men to prepare their own in the bunkhouse.

Charlie, though, had insisted Annie cook a full breakfast, dinner and supper for the men. It was just another of his many ways of keeping her in her place, of reminding her who was boss.

She had never minded spending time in the kitchen when it was voluntary. But because he was forcing her to do it, she had grown to hate it. Her cooking responsibilities had become symbolic of the mess she had created for herself.

Freeing herself from the kitchen had been almost as liberating as freeing herself from her sham of a marriage. Maybe it was a true sign of how far she had come that she had started to once more enjoy cooking on the nights when it was her turn.

Most of the time she enjoyed these evening meals, she corrected her earlier thought. This one wasn't exactly the most comfortable of suppers. Leah said nothing, just glowered at everyone and picked at her food. None of the other men seemed in the mood for conversation and if not for C.J.'s constant chatter to Joe about his day, they all would have eaten in silence.

Finally Luke Mitchell wiped his mouth with his napkin and cleared his throat. "Tastes delicious, Miz Redhawk. As usual." He must have finally worked up the nerve to speak, and he punctuated the compliment with a shy, eager smile across the table.

Out of the corner of her gaze, she saw Ruben and Manny exchange grins and she felt a flush of embarrassment begin at the nape of her neck and spread up.

She was really going to have to do something about
him, and soon.

"Thank you," she murmured.

"I mean it," he persisted. "You make a real good
spaghetti sauce."

The fact that it was her night to cook had completely
slipped her mind until she had returned from the barn
after delivering the calf. She hadn't had time to do much
more than open a jar of store-bought sauce and mix it
with ground beef, but she didn't want to embarrass the
eager ranch hand by pointing out the obvious so she
just smiled politely.

"With that wind chill, we're supposed to dip down
to minus twenty tonight," Joe interjected before Luke
could say anything else. "That means we're going to
have to drop another load of hay after dinner. Mitchell,
you and I can take the cows and calves up on the winter
range. Manny, Ruben, you can take care of the bulls
and yearlings down by the creek. Patch, can you handle
the animals in the barns by yourself?"

The grizzled old cowboy nodded. For the next several
moments, Annie listened with only half an ear to them
discuss ranch business and the constant struggle to keep
the livestock warm for the night. The rest of her waited,
nerves twitching like a calf on locoweed, for Joe to tell
everyone he was leaving.

He seemed to want to drag it out, though, while they
discussed vaccinations and the yearly race to be the first
ranch in the area to have the calving over with and how
many of last year's steers they would take to auction in
a few weeks.

She waited all through dinner but it was only after
the men cleared their plates and she had dished up left-

over apple pie for dessert that Joe set his fork down with a clatter and pushed back his chair.

"I have an announcement," he began. Damn. This was harder than he expected it to be. As he studied the faces around the table, his gut clenched and he scrambled for words.

"I'm, uh…I'm leaving the Double C," he finally just said bluntly. "I'll be taking a new job in Wyoming come April."

Everyone was silent for several moments. He saw varying degrees of shock on everyone's expression except Annie's—from profound surprise in Patch's good eye to what he could only describe as an odd kind of glee on Luke Mitchell's smooth-cheeked features.

To his surprise, Leah was the first to react—Leah, who acted like she couldn't stand him most of the time. She slid her chair back from the table so abruptly it tipped backward as she stood. She didn't bother to right it again, just looked at him out of dark eyes wounded with an expression of complete betrayal, like he'd suddenly up and slapped her for no reason, then she rushed out of the kitchen.

The sound of her pounding up the stairs seemed to break the spell for all of them and everyone began talking at once.

"You're gonna run out right in the middle of planting season?" Patch exclaimed.

"Where in Wyoming are you going?" Ruben asked.

"I guess that means Miz Redhawk's gonna need to find herself a new foreman," Luke said.

It was C.J.'s plaintive cry that pierced through the buzz of questions, and brought the men's conversation to a grinding halt. "You can't leave, too, Uncle Joe! You *can't!*"

Awkward silence echoed through the kitchen while he scrambled for something to say to make things right. Before he could figure out a way to achieve the impossible, Patch cleared his throat, discomfort plain on his face. "Uh, boys, we've got some feed to put out if we want to spend the worst of that storm out there where it's warm and dry. There'll be time to talk about this later."

Eager to avoid the scene they all must have known was inevitable, the men murmured their thanks to Annie for the meal then trooped out of the kitchen, leaving him alone with her and her son.

The boy was trying valiantly not to cry but a tear trickled from the corner of his eye anyway, leaving a watery path down the side of his nose. His fingers trembled as he swiped at it, damn near breaking Joe's heart.

"C.J.—"

Whatever he was going to say was lost as C.J. cut him off. "You promised you'd take me campin' and fishin' on the Ruby this summer. You *promised!*"

He flashed a look toward Annie and found her watching her son out of green eyes filled with compassion and pain.

"We can still go." His voice sounded hoarse. "I'll try to get away for a weekend and come up and take you."

"It won't be the same."

"I know. I'm sorry."

More tears followed the pathway of that lone trailblazer and Joe felt small and mean for putting them there. He wanted to gather his nephew close, to try to absorb his pain into him if he could, but he sensed the boy would only jerk away.

"Just because I'm leaving doesn't mean I'll stop being your uncle," he said quietly. "That'll never change. We can still talk on the phone and write letters. I promise, I'll take you on that fishing trip this summer and maybe you can even come stay with me for a while once I get settled."

"It won't be the same," C.J. cried again. His whole face crumpled. "Why do you have to go?"

How could he explain to a seven-year-old how a man sometimes ached for more than he had, more than he would ever have? And how sometimes the lack of it, this constant, aching emptiness, was like a living thing chewing away at him until he couldn't breathe?

C.J. didn't wait for an answer, which was probably a good thing since he didn't have one to offer. The boy stared up at him, and there was a world of disillusionment in his eyes. "You're no different than *him*. I thought you were, but you're not."

The impassioned words—and all the heartbreak behind it—sliced into him like a just-sharpened blade. *No different than him.* Than Charlie. The man who had spent every one of C.J.'s seven years destroying his faith in everything.

It was his greatest fear—that he and his half brother were more alike than he wanted to believe. That somehow the genetic makeup they had in common was stronger than his own self-control.

They weren't, he reminded himself. He had done his damnedest throughout his life to make sure of that. Charlie was a drunk and a bully who delighted in terrorizing anybody smaller than he was. He wasn't anything like him.

Oh no, he thought with sudden bitterness. Nothing at all. He was just an ex-con who served four years in Deer Lodge for killing his father.

He thrust the thought away and tried to concentrate on the crisis at hand. "C.J.—" he began, but the boy turned away.

"If you leave, I don't want you to come back. I don't want to go to the Ruby with you. I don't want to go *anywhere* with you." And for the second time in just a few minutes, the room echoed with the sound of feet pounding up the stairs and the slam of a bedroom door.

At the sound, Annie froze for just an instant, then she stood abruptly and started clearing away dishes with quick, jerky movements, as if she was suddenly desperate to keep her hands busy.

He scratched his cheek. "That went well, don't you think?"

She fumbled with a plate, catching it just in time to keep it from smashing to the floor, and sent him a baleful look. "Great. Just great. With all these slamming doors, I'm surprised none of the windows are broken."

His laugh sounded raw and strained. "I'm sorry, Annie. I didn't think they'd take it this hard."

"They love you," she said simply. "You've always been decent and kind to them. Lord knows, they got little enough of that from their…from Charlie."

"I hate like hell that I'm putting them through this."

"They'll live. People get over all kinds of things."

Have you? He wanted to ask, but didn't. He carried a pile of plates to the sink, wishing things were different. That he didn't have to leave. That these were his dishes, that this was his kitchen.

That she was his woman.

Chapter 3

What a mess.

With her hands curled around a mug of lemon tea, Annie sighed and looked out the kitchen window at the snow whirled around by the shrieking wind. Hours after Joe's announcement at dinner, her head still ached, her nerves still in an uproar, and nothing seemed to help.

C.J. was finally asleep after crying most of the evening. She had a feeling if she checked his pillowcase, it would be damp with more tears.

He couldn't understand why the man who had been more of a father to him in the last eighteen months than his own father had been for his whole life could just walk away. All her efforts to console him only seemed to sound hollow and trite.

She had knocked on Leah's door a few minutes earlier to tell her to turn the lights out and had received just a grunt in return. Her daughter was no longer speaking to her, but she didn't know if it was due to Joe's impending departure or because of their earlier battle over homework and riding privileges.

Had she been this difficult when she was twelve? She didn't think so. She had been a handful, certainly, always tumbling into trouble with Joe and Colt, but she'd always tried hard not to disappoint her father, anxious for the love he had such a hard time demonstrating.

Of course, by the time she was twelve, Joe and Colt had been in high school and too busy with sports and school and girls to pay much attention to the wild-haired tomboy from the ranch next door who used to follow them everywhere.

She sighed again. If she didn't stop woolgathering, she was going to be up all night trying to finish this blasted help-wanted ad. She wanted to be able to call it into the newspaper and some of the ranch periodicals in the morning.

She read what she'd written so far: "Wanted: Experienced foreman to oversee six-hundred-head Hereford operation. Prefer long-term commitment and extensive ranching background. Salary based on experience. Must be loyal and hard-working."

She winced. Was she advertising for a foreman or a dog? She scribbled the last part out and was trying to come up with something better when she heard a soft knock at the back door.

A quick glance at the clock over the stove showed it was nearly ten—a little late for company.

Maybe Joe had some unfinished ranch business he needed to discuss. It wasn't unusual for him to stop by after the evening chores were done to talk about what needed to be done the next day—a gesture she appreciated but which she'd tried to tell him repeatedly wasn't necessary. She trusted his instincts completely.

It would take a long time to build up that kind of trust with whomever she finally hired to replace him. She set the pencil down so hard the lead snapped off, and went to answer the door.

To her surprise, it wasn't Joe she found in the light of the back porch at all but Luke Mitchell, looking nervous and edgy and, if possible, even younger than normal.

"Luke! Is something wrong?"

"No. I just…" the ranch hand shifted his weight, "I wanted to talk to you tonight. Are you busy?"

"No. Just trying to write an ad for a new foreman. Come in."

She helped brush snow off his black slicker in the mudroom, then led the way into the kitchen. "Can I get you something? I was having a cup of tea and there's plenty more hot water."

He shook his head. The movement seemed to remind him of his manners because he abruptly yanked the cowboy hat from his head, leaving a flat line haloing his blond hair.

She took her seat again and pointed to another chair. "Why don't you sit down, then."

He shook his head again, a quick, restless gesture. Shoulders tense, he stood in the doorway and began measuring the brim of his hat with his fingers. Round and round he went, first in one direction then the other, over and over until—given her lingering headache and the uproar of her emotions—she had to fight the urge to yank the blasted thing away from him and throw it on the table.

He opened his mouth to speak twice, but both times he jerked it shut again, and she could tell he was trying to work up his nerve for some kind of major announcement.

Fiddlesticks. She had absolutely no energy left to deal with this after the day she'd had. "It's late," she finally said, when it looked like he was going to stand in her kitchen fidgeting all night. She should probably try to be more patient, but she just wasn't in the mood tonight. "What can I do for you, Luke?"

"I'd like to apply for the foreman job," he blurted out, so loudly it startled both of them.

The foreman job? She stared at him, shocked, watching a flush creep up those baby-smooth cheeks. Of all the possibilities racing through her head about what he might be doing there at ten o'clock at night, the idea that he wanted Joe's job never would have occurred to her.

"I know I'm young and all but I'm a hard worker. Joe's always sayin' so. I'm strong and I'm willing and I've been around cattle all my life. If my daddy hadn't had lost our spread because of the damn banks—excuse my language, ma'am—I'd be on my way to runnin' my own place by now."

Like so many ranching families, the Mitchells had been hurt by the recent run of low beef prices. They had run a pretty big spread near Big Sky and she knew his father slightly.

She heard he was trying to support his large family by working in a ranch supply store over in Bozeman now. It had been one of the reasons she'd taken a chance and hired Luke two months earlier, in an effort to give the family one less mouth to feed.

Compassion for the eager young man washed over her. To grow up thinking he would take over the reins of the family ranch someday and then to lose it all with the bang of an auctioneer's gavel must have been devastating. Heaven knows, it was one of her own biggest fears.

"You could do a whole lot worse, ma'am," Luke went on, "if you don't mind me sayin'."

Drat Joe for putting her in this position. She rubbed suddenly clammy hands on her jeans beneath the table. The last thing she wanted to do was hurt his fragile pride by telling him she didn't think he was man enough for the job.

Especially when life had already dealt him a rough hand—and when he had more than a slight crush on her. "I... You've been a real asset to the Double C, Luke."

"Thank you." His wide grin made him look not much older than C.J. "I could be even more of an asset as foreman. I have some real good ideas about improving things around here. Not that Joe hasn't done a good job, mind, but I've been reading about these fancy new low-cholesterol breeds they got out there and I think it might be worth your while to look into it."

He went on for several minutes about the direction he'd like to take the Double C. She listened with only half an ear, trying to figure out how she could let him down gently. Finally she realized he had wound down and was waiting expectantly for an answer.

She cleared her throat. "I have to say, those certainly sound like interesting ideas."

"Does that mean you're willing to give me a chance?"

She paused, feeling like she was about to drop-kick a puppy, then finally drew in a deep breath and took aim. "Luke, you're a good cowhand. Like you said, you're a hard worker, always willing to dig in and do what has to be done, no matter what. And while I'll certainly keep you in mind for the foreman's job, I have to be honest with you. I was hoping for somebody with a little more experience.''

''I told you, I've been around cattle all my life. That's twenty years of experience right there.''

Twenty years. Oh mercy. He wasn't even as old as she had thought he was. She felt like a shriveled up old lady compared to all this youthful exuberance.

''It's more than just experience.''

She fumbled for words for a few moments, then decided she would just have to be blunt, as much as she hated it, and as much as it might hurt. ''The foreman of a ranch like the Double C has to have a certain…authority. Not just with the hands who work on the ranch, but out in the community, too—with other ranchers, with our suppliers, when we take stock to auction. He has to be able to command respect in the ranching community and that's something that comes not just with experience, but with age.''

And something Joe still struggled with, at least with the ranchers around Madison Valley who couldn't forget his history. She frowned, wondering if that was one of the reasons he was leaving, if he thought his presence was somehow detrimental to the Double C's bottom line.

''So what you're sayin' is you're not gonna hire me because I'm too young?'' The boy couldn't have looked more offended if she had just told him his horse was ugly.

''I'm not saying you could never be foreman of the Double C,'' she answered. ''But I have to be honest with you. I just don't know if it's a responsibility you're ready for yet.''

Hurt flickered in his pale blue eyes and with it she glimpsed a deep anger that somehow made him look much older. Just as quickly, the anger disappeared and she wondered if she had imagined it.

"I see." His voice was low in the hushed kitchen, so quiet she could barely hear him. "So that's it?"

She nodded. "I'm sorry, Luke. I'd like nothing better than to hire you for the job right now. Maybe in a few more years, though."

"You're wrong." Though he spoke in the same quiet, intense voice, he gripped his hat so hard it creased the soft brown felt. He shoved the hat on his head. "I could do a helluva lot better job than Redhawk. I could prove it to you if you'd only give me a chance."

He didn't wait for an answer but stalked out of the kitchen and into the storm.

She watched through the window as he made his way back to the bunkhouse, shoulders hunched against the wind and whirling snow. Just as he went inside the doublewide trailer he shared with Patch and the Santiago brothers, a flicker of movement near the barn caught her gaze.

The vapor light on the power pole between the house and the outbuildings wasn't powerful enough to completely pierce the darkness or the whirling snow, but she thought she could just make out the figure of a man standing motionless, his attention focused on her, on the house.

For just an instant, her heart stuttered, and old feelings of dread and helplessness came roiling back, and then the figure moved out of the shadows and she recognized Joe's black Stetson and broad shoulders. Unlike Luke, he walked unbent in the wind, oblivious to the storm raging around him as he came toward the house.

"Everything okay in here?" he asked after she opened the door off the mudroom to his knock.

She shrugged. "Why wouldn't it be?"

"I saw Mitchell walking back to the trailer. Just wanted to make sure he wasn't pestering you."

"Pestering me?"

He cocked his head. "I told you at supper, it's no secret the boy's got it bad, Annie. He makes moon-eyes at you every time he gets within spitting distance. I wouldn't want him to make a nuisance of himself."

She felt herself blush. "I can handle it."

"Well, let me know if he gets to be too much of a bother and I'll have a word with him."

Why did he always assume she couldn't take care of things by herself? Probably because she had a pretty lousy track record in that department, she admitted.

"He wasn't pestering me or making moon-eyes or anything like that. If you must know, he was applying for your job."

For a long moment, he just stared at her, the only sound in the kitchen the ticking of the clock and the whirring of the furnace spewing warm air out of the register, then he tilted back his head and laughed, low and long and deep.

The sound of it—so rare coming from him—slid over her nerve endings like silk.

"He wants to be foreman?" He laughed again and flipped a chair around to straddle it, removing his hat and tossing it onto the table in the same motion. "I hope you didn't encourage him."

There he went again, thinking she didn't have a brain in her head. "Of course I didn't. I told him I was looking for somebody with a little more experience."

He snorted. "I'm sure that went over well."

"About like you'd expect."

"How could he think you'd be willing to hire a twenty-year-old kid to run a big operation like the Double C?"

"Maybe he thought I'd be desperate, with you leaving and all."

He studied her for a moment, then looked away. "How's the boy?"

"Sleeping. Finally."

"I hate like hell that I hurt him like this."

"Of course he's hurting! Did you think you could just walk away and it wouldn't affect any of us?"

"I guess I was hoping it wouldn't."

"You're part of the Double C, Joe. More than that, you're part of this family. What you do affects all of us. C.J. loves you—of course he's upset you're going to leave. And Leah is, too, although she shows it differently."

"What about you? Are you upset I'm leaving?"

He didn't know why he asked it. Maybe because she looked so damn beautiful here in her warm, cozy kitchen, with the light from above the stove turning her hair red-gold and making her eyes look soft and welcoming and her mouth about the sexiest thing he'd ever seen.

Or maybe because he'd been more annoyed than he had a right to be when he saw Mitchell sneaking out her back door so late at night.

Whatever his reason for asking, her answer was clear. "You know I am." She spoke in a low voice and then lifted eyes the color of brand-new aspen leaves to his.

He was shocked to his bones at the depth of emotion there—if he didn't know better, he could swear there were tears lurking in those green depths, but Annie hardly ever cried.

Even if she *had* been the watering-pot sort, his brother would have fixed that in a hurry.

He reached out and grabbed her hand. It was rougher than it should have been, almost as nicked-up and callused as his own. She was killing herself trying to turn the Double C back into the ranch it once was. And he sure didn't help matters any by taking off.

Her fingers trembled in his and he realized too late why he did his best to avoid touching her—just the simple contact of her hand in his filled him with wants and needs he had absolutely no business wanting or needing.

What would she do if he reached across that scarred pine table and pulled her to him, if he dug his fingers into that sinful hair and devoured that luscious mouth of hers like he imagined doing a dozen times a day?

Easy. More than likely, she'd kick him off the ranch herself. She'd barely survived being tangled up with one Redhawk brother and she sure didn't need the other one messing things up for her now.

But wasn't he doing just that by taking this job in Wyoming? Putting her to the trouble of having to find a new foreman and leaving her to deal with two upset kids?

He shifted on the hard chair. "Maybe I ought to just call Waterson and tell him to forget it."

Relief flickered in her eyes for just a moment, then she shook her head vigorously. "I won't let you do that. You've sacrificed enough of your life for us. You're right, you need to move on and this sounds like a wonderful opportunity for you, a real chance to make a new start. It will be good for you. And whether we like it or not, it will be good for us not to depend on you so much.''

She was ready to cut him loose, he thought as he said his goodbyes a few moments later and headed back out into the blizzard. So why was he suddenly not so sure he wanted to be free?

She was becoming a pretty darn good liar.

Her conversation with Joe the night before ran through her head over and over while she tried to catch up on the mounds of paperwork that seemed to pile up like January snow.

Since the kids were still in school and the men were out repairing damage from the storm the night before, she had the ranch house to herself. She should have been able to make a real dent in that month's bills, but she couldn't seem to concentrate on much of anything.

On anything except a dark-eyed Shoshone who would be blowing out of her life on the last of the winter storms.

She sighed and forced herself to concentrate on all the work she had to do. It wasn't doing her any good to brood about Joe's leaving. If she didn't stop it, she would be completely worthless for the two remaining months she had left with him.

She was just wincing over the check she had to write to the vet when the door off the mudroom suddenly creaked open, sounding abnormally loud in the stillness of the empty house. Just as abruptly, it closed again with a quiet click.

She glanced at the digital clock on the command line of the computer. Odd. The kids weren't due home from school for several hours and Joe said he thought the men would be tied up most of the day fixing the roof of the hay shed in the far pasture. They'd taken lunch with them but maybe they forgot something or finished up earlier than expected.

"Hello?" she called out. "I'm back here in the office."

She was met by silence, unbroken except for the low, ubiquitous whir of the furnace. A shiver sneaked down her spine and she frowned. "Hello?" she called again.

No one answered.

Was somebody playing some of kind of trick on her? She didn't think any of the men had that kind of cruel streak in them, but Patch could be mischievous and his sense of humor sometimes veered off into warped territory.

Puzzled, she rose from the computer and walked out of the office, through the empty family room and toward the kitchen at the other side of the house. In the thick silence, her pulse sounded loud and strident in her ears. She was more edgy than she cared to admit, a realization that sent fresh anger coursing through her.

This house, with its softly weathered logs and its wraparound porch, was her haven now. She had no reason to be afraid here anymore and she hated that someone could dredge up all these old feelings. If it was Patch playing a trick, she planned to give him an earful he wouldn't soon forget.

She walked into the big kitchen, expecting somebody to jump out any minute with a gleeful "boo," but the room was empty.

She scratched the back of her head, baffled and uneasy. Was she going crazy? She *had* heard the door open and close, hadn't she?

Maybe not. Maybe she was hearing things. Maybe

she was just overwrought from all the stress of the day before.

It was the only explanation, since there was obviously no one in the house and a quick glance out the kitchen window showed no one between the house and the out-buildings except a few chickens scratching through the snow looking for lunch.

She couldn't see any tracks on the walk either, but C.J. had cleared most of the snow away this morning and the rest was so packed it probably wouldn't show anything.

This was too creepy. Maybe she ought to go take a look upstairs....

The phone suddenly jangled loudly in the silence, sending her jumping at least a foot into the air. She grabbed at her chest where her heart threatened to hammer through her rib cage. "It's just the phone, you big baby," she chided herself, and crossed to the wall unit next to the refrigerator.

"Hello?" Despite her best efforts to calm herself, her pulse still fluttered wildly.

"Hey. I hear you're on the lookout for a new fore-man."

She slumped against the counter at the familiar voice of her closest neighbor and pushed away the rest of her lingering unease. "Hey, Colt. News travels fast."

"It does when it's bad news. What the hell is Joe thinking? He can't leave you in the lurch like that, right before spring planting."

"He's given me two months' notice—more than any-one else would. I can't ask for more than that."

"I can. I'm coming over to talk some sense into him."

She ground her teeth. Lord spare her from arrogant

men who didn't think she was competent enough to brush her teeth without them standing over her checking every last inch of enamel.

Colton McKendrick grew up on the adjacent ranch, the Broken Spur, where Joe's father had worked. And just like Joe, he thought it was his mission in life to watch out for her. Even though she had been four years younger than the boys, they were the only other kids for miles so the three of them had been inseparable, always tumbling into one scrape after another.

Before her divorce, Joe had run the Broken Spur for him while Colt devoted himself first to the military and then to FBI undercover work, trying to outrun his ghosts.

She loved him dearly and was thrilled that his days of running were over, but she wished just once he and Joe would both realize she was all grown up and could take care of herself.

Most of the time, anyway.

"Colt, stay out of it. This is something Joe wants to do and I've accepted that. You should, too."

"Bull. You need him."

"I need a foreman," she answered. "But it doesn't necessarily have to be Joe Redhawk."

"He's the best there is. Dammit, how can he just run out on you like this?"

"You'll have to ask him that."

"I plan to, right now. I'm on my way."

Colt severed the connection before she could argue with him. She had barely returned the phone to the receiver and put more coffee on when she heard the crunch of truck tires on snow out front, followed by a vehicle door slamming.

She opened the mudroom door before he could knock

and was pleased to see Colt helping his very pregnant wife up the walk.

"What did you do, call from the mailbox?" she teased when they were safely inside.

"Just about. Aren't cellular phones something?" He grinned and pulled her into a quick hug.

When he released her, she turned to his wife. "No office hours today, Maggie?"

"I don't have any patients scheduled until this afternoon since I had my own appointment with Dr. Marcus."

"And what did he say?"

"Everything's fine. He moved my due date up to mid-April. It won't be a moment too soon, as far as I'm concerned. I feel as big as one of those Herefords out there."

Annie smiled. Colt and Maggie had married just weeks after her divorce and in the time since, she had come to love Colt's sweetly elegant wife almost as much as she did him. There was a bond between the two women, forged of shared pain and rare understanding.

"You look absolutely radiant," Annie said.

"Everybody always says that to fat old pregnant women."

"Because it's true." It was. Maggie's eyes were soft, serene, and her skin glowed with an inner tranquility that had to come from knowing her husband adored her and was thrilled about the child they had created together.

For just a moment, Annie tasted bitter envy in her mouth. She hadn't experienced that contentment with either of her pregnancies. Instead, she had known only that trapped, powerless fear.

Dammit. She wanted to pinch herself, hard. Couldn't she even be happy for two of her closest friends in the world over the upcoming birth of their child without this blasted self-pity taking over? She had two beautiful children, a ranch some men would kill for, and good friends like the McKendricks. Why couldn't she let that be enough?

"Where's Joe?" Colt asked.

She swallowed the envy and poured coffee, black the way he liked it. Maggie, she knew, was staying away from caffeine for the baby's sake, so she put water on to boil for herbal tea.

"We lost the roof on one of the hay sheds in the wind last night," she answered. "The men are doing their best to patch it together. What about the Broken Spur? How did you fare in the storm?"

"Lost three calves but it could have been a lot worse." He sipped his coffee. "Now suppose you tell me what burr Joe's got in his britches about taking some fool job in Wyoming."

She busied herself rifling through the cupboard for the tea bags. "It sounds like a good opportunity for him."

"What does he think he's going to find at some stranger's ranch in Wyoming that he can't get in Madison Valley?"

"You'll have to ask him that," she said quietly.

"I'm asking you. What happened between you two?"

"Nothing." She shut the cupboard door with a little more force than necessary. "Absolutely nothing. Why would you think that? Things are just fine between us."

Unless you count the way he couldn't stand to touch

her and the way he sometimes went out of his way to avoid even looking at her.

"So why is he in such a big hurry to leave?"

She thought of those moments in the barn the day before and that rare vulnerability she had glimpsed in Joe.

Would she be breaking a confidence to talk to Colt about it? No. Colt cared about Joe. The two men shared a friendship closer than blood. Maybe if he knew the truth, Colt wouldn't push him to stay against his will.

She almost laughed. Was she really going out of her way to defend Joe for taking a new job? Yes. She wanted him to stay, but she wanted him to find peace more. "He has a chance to start his own herd and to buy land of his own. I can't match this Waterson's offer, and I'm not sure I would even if I had the means."

"Why the hell not?"

"Colt, he told me he wants to start over some place away from Madison Valley." She paused. "Somewhere he can be just another rancher, just like everybody else."

He was silent for a moment, his mouth set in a hard line, then he swore softly, pungently. "How can we argue with that?"

"Exactly."

"I don't understand," Maggie interjected with a frown.

Colt turned to his wife. "You know what it's like for him in town. How people talk. He tries to pretend it doesn't matter, but it obviously affects him more than any of us thought."

The kettle whistled suddenly, shrilly, and Annie rose from the table to pour water for Maggie's tea. "It just makes me so mad," she muttered. "Why can't people forget, just stop judging him for what happened years ago, for heaven's sake? Why can't they look at the man he's made of himself?''

''We don't have all that many murders around here, Annie. Of course people are going to remember it.''

''It wasn't murder and you know it! And so does everybody else in town.''

''Not everybody. There are a lot of people who think Joe killed his father in cold blood and got off easy.''

In cold blood. It was an odd term to use for something as violent as taking the life of another human being.

''It was an accident.'' She couldn't help her vehemence, even though she knew she was preaching to the choir. ''That's why he pleaded guilty to involuntary manslaughter. The only reason he served prison time at all was because he had alcohol in his system, even though it was under the legal limit, and because he was already on probation for that stupid bar fight when he was just a kid. Everybody with a brain in his head knows Joe was trying to protect his mother after Al beat her half to death.''

''You've heard the rumors that there was more to it than that.''

Yes, and she knew exactly who was behind them. She frowned. Charlie had kept his promise after he married her and hadn't gone to his boss at the sheriff's department with his version of events that night. But he hadn't had any qualms whipping up the rumor mill in town.

Just another sin to lay at the door of her ex-husband.

She knew Joe hadn't meant to kill his father when he had delivered that fateful punch. But even if he *had,* Albert Redhawk deserved everything he got and more.

He had spent his whole life and two marriages physically and emotionally abusing his entire family, turning one son into a mirror image of himself and the other into a stoic little boy who buried all his emotions so deeply it took nothing short of a cataclysmic event to ever bring them gushing out.

"It's funny what people choose to remember of the dead." Colt's low voice jolted her back to the conversation. "Selective memory, I guess. Al was a real son of a bitch to just about everybody, but if you listened to some people in town, you'd think he was the next best thing to Santa Claus."

"Is it any wonder Joe wants to make a fresh start somewhere else."

"I guess." Colt sipped his coffee glumly. "So what are we gonna do about it?"

She rested a hand on his shoulder. "Nothing we *can* do. Just miss him, I suppose. Just miss him."

Colt and Maggie didn't stay long after that, only long enough to finish their coffee and tea. When she had the house to herself again, she forced herself to stay in the office until she could make inroads toward finishing her paperwork.

The mysterious door opening completely slipped her mind until hours later, after Leah and C.J. came home, strewing their customary clutter throughout the mudroom and kitchen.

She was picking up backpacks and mittens and school books when she saw what looked like a white square of paper under one of C.J.'s wet boots near the back door. She gave an exasperated sigh. It was probably a permission slip for a school field trip or something equally important.

She lifted the boot away and picked up the soggy paper, then felt her whole body go stiff and cold.

It wasn't a permission slip at all, but a photograph.

A Polaroid taken through her office window that afternoon, of her sitting behind her desk doing paperwork.

Chapter 4

Something was wrong.

Joe sat at the kitchen table watching Annie bounce from the table to the stove to the refrigerator then back to the table like some out-of-control mechanical toy on an endless track.

Something was definitely wrong.

He'd noticed it all through dinner. She hardly touched her food and her face was so pale her little sprinkling of freckles stood out in stark relief.

Every few minutes she would pause from shifting her food back and forth on her plate and gaze out the window, her eyes wide and frantic as she searched the early-evening darkness, looking for what, he couldn't even begin to guess.

No one else seemed aware of her unease. Leah and C.J. both sat sullen and silent, ignoring him to the point of rudeness, and the rest of the men were too tired from the long day of cleaning the mess from the storm to pay attention to much of anything but their food.

He noticed, though, just as he noticed everything she did. Something had her more high-strung than a thoroughbred in a barn full of snakes and he couldn't even begin to guess what it might be.

Wood squeaked on linoleum as Leah suddenly pushed her chair back, jolting him from his thoughts. "May I be excused?"

Annie turned from the window. She blinked a few times, then focused on her daughter. "I…yes. What's the status of your homework?"

Leah's mouth tightened. "Almost done."

"As soon as it's finished, bring it down so we can go over it together."

"I said I was almost done. Don't you believe me?"

Despite whatever was bothering her, Annie's voice was calm in marked contrast to her daughter's. "It's not a matter of me believing you. I would just like to try to help you by checking your answers. We have the same goal here. As soon as you get your grades back up, you can regain your riding privileges. That's what you want, isn't it?"

Leah's look fell just shy of a glare. "Whatever," she said shortly, then hurried from the room.

As soon as she left, C.J. set his fork down on his plate with a loud clatter and looked past Joe toward his mother. "May I be excused, too?"

Annie nodded distractedly and didn't even chide C.J. when he went into the family room and turned on the television set without clearing away his plate.

The children's departure seemed to signal the end of the meal. Patch and the rest of the men scraped their plates clean just a few moments later and rose to leave.

Luke Mitchell paused by the table. "Real fine dinner again, Miz Redhawk. Just about the best beef pie I've ever had."

His words didn't seem to register for a moment, then she shook her head. "Beef pie is Patch's specialty. It was his night to cook."

"Oh. Well, it was real good. Good night."

She was busy looking out the window again and didn't answer him. Luke finally shoved his hat back on his head and stalked out the door.

The compliment to Annie was the most genial Joe had seen him all day. The kid had had been brooding and sour since breakfast.

If Annie hadn't told him about Luke applying for the foreman's the night before, Joe might have been tempted to rip into him for his rotten attitude, but he decided to give him a little leeway just this once.

He figured the kid had some right to his foul mood. When the woman of your heart turned you down for a job, it was bound to stick in your craw. Still, if things didn't improve in the morning, he might need to sit the kid down for a little serious one-on-one.

He was still reflecting on what a pain in the neck employee relations could be when he realized everybody else had taken off and he and Annie were alone in the kitchen.

She stood suddenly and began silently clearing the table. Her jerky movements reminded him of the way she used to scurry around trying to do her best to make herself invisible around Charlie, so much that an eerie chill skulked down his spine.

He stood it as long as he could then clamped his teeth together and rose to his feet. He cursed the abrupt motion almost as soon as he made it when she jumped like a startled mare.

He'd worked hard after Charlie left not to move too suddenly around her. Not to speak too loudly, not to gesture too much, not to do anything else her subconscious might interpret as a threat. Over the last eighteen months she had lost much of her edginess, but sometimes it reemerged.

Like tonight.

"Sorry," he muttered, feeling the hot ball of rage explode in his gut like it always did whenever he thought about what his brother had done to her. He drew several sharp breaths until he forced it down. "Didn't mean to spook you."

"It's not you," she said distractedly.

"What, then?"

"Nothing."

"Come on, Annie. What's wrong?"

She fiddled with the stack of plates in her hand. "What makes you think something's wrong?"

"Well, let's see. For starters, you've been more quiet than a barn mouse, then you jump if anybody so much as looks at you wrong, and to top it all off, you don't say a single word to Leah when she skips out on her night to do dishes."

She winced and glanced at the chart hanging on the refrigerator. "It was her night, wasn't it?"

"I'm guessing that's why she was in such a rush to get back to her homework."

She blew out a breath. "I should probably make her come down and take her turn, shouldn't I?"

With that reluctance in the green of her eyes, it was obvious the idea appealed to her about as much as an

IRS audit. He shrugged. "I'm afraid this really isn't my area of expertise. You're the mother here."

She flashed him a quick, unreadable look then focused on the stack of plates in her hands. "Right. I'm really not up to another battle tonight. Sometimes it's just easier to just do things myself. Does that make me a terrible mother?"

"No. You're not a terrible mother. Give yourself a break, Annie. You're a tired mother. Why don't you let me do these?"

"No, I'm fine. Thanks, anyway."

She would argue into the night if he let her, so Joe just went to work clearing the rest of the dishes from the table then filling the sink with soapy water. He started washing the dishes and a few moments later she joined him with a towel to dry.

They worked in silence for a few moments. He was painfully aware of the way she smelled sweetly, innocently, of apples. No matter how hard he tried to block it out it reached him even over the lemony scent of the dish soap.

He scrubbed hard at a dish, annoyed with himself.

"So are you going to tell me what's got you so jumpy?" he asked to distract himself.

She focused on the plate in her hand. "Just the wind, I guess," she mumbled. "Sometimes it gets to me."

Since when? he wanted to ask, but held his tongue, knowing damn well she wouldn't answer.

The old Annie had always loved wild weather. When they were kids, she never wanted to be cooped up indoors during summer storms. With the same kind of giddy delight other girls her age reserved for the latest heartthrob, she would sit out on the wide porch at the big house while the sky flashed and growled around her.

One time when she was about twelve, she was tagging along after Colt and him while they went looking for strays up near Lone Eagle Peak. Halfway up the mountain, they had been surprised by an afternoon thunder bumper and like any sensible teenagers, he and Colt had rushed to find cover under an overhanging rock formation.

He could still remember turning around to find Annie, her wild red curls already plastered to her head, standing out in the rain. With her arms wide and her face lifted to the sky in supplication, she looked like some kind of mystical creature from a storybook.

He remembered gazing at her, entranced, until lightning scorched an old pine no more than a hundred yards away. Then Joe had finally braved the pelting rain to yank her to safety.

The old Annie had thrived on the power and majesty of mountain storms. Had his brother taken that from her, too?

That ball of fury hissed and seethed to life in his gut again as he thought of how that laughing, crazy, courageous girl had changed. He allowed the anger to writhe around for only a few seconds but before it could slither out, he inhaled a sharp breath and caged it again. Venting his anger only upset her more and left him feeling hollow and achy.

With effort, he turned his thoughts away from the grim ghosts of the past and focused on something more benign. "When I was up on the roof of the hay shed, I thought I saw Colt's pickup coming down the road."

She nodded. "He and Maggie dropped by on the way home from a doctor's appointment."

"Everything okay with the baby?"

"I think so. The doctor moved up her due date, to mid-April. She looked wonderful."

He had thought so too the last time he'd seen Colt and Maggie, and had been filled with a sense of loss so profound it had stunned him. He would never share that kind of magic, never watch a woman he loved grow huge with his child, and the realization had hit him in the chest like a hard fist.

He had decided a long time ago that he would never marry, had resigned himself to going it alone for the rest of his life. What choice did he have? He didn't have a whole hell of a lot to offer a woman, not considering the kind of family he came from.

What woman would want a convicted murderer, especially one who came from a legacy of violence and abuse?

He thought he had accepted the way things had to be. But seeing Colt and Maggie so excited about bringing a new life into the world had made his own life seem hollow in comparison.

Yet another of the many reasons driving him toward making a fresh start away from here.

"So why did they stop in?" he asked abruptly. "Just for coffee?"

She took the last pan out of the rinse water without looking at him. "Colt heard about your new job. He came over all worked up, ready to horsewhip you for deserting me."

He shouldn't feel this guilt seeping through him like spring runoff, dammit. He had to learn to let go. How was he going to carve out a new life for himself when he feared he would never be completely free of the old one? "So why didn't he?"

Before she could figure out how to answer, a dog's

angry barking cut through the low, distant moan of the wind. The pan she was drying slipped from her hand, landing harmlessly in the sink. She paid it no attention as she strained to search the menacing shadows out the window.

"What is it?" Joe asked.

"I...I'm not sure. Dolly's barking at something."

"Probably just a couple of deer looking for food."

She barely heard him as her gaze swept the fence line, the spruce windbreak, the drifts of snow covering her garden. Whoever snapped that picture of her was out there somewhere. She could feel it deep in her bones. He was out there watching her, taunting her....

All evening she had struggled to contain her reaction to seeing that photograph of herself taken by some unknown person watching her through the window. Now, though, it finally broke through her fragile barriers and crashed over her in wave after wave of paralyzing panic.

Someone had been watching her. While she had worked at her paperwork completely unaware, someone had been just a thin sheet of glass away. Watching her.

How long had he stood outside the window?

And why?

As soon as she felt the fear begin to take over, felt the return of that helplessness she hated so much, she stiffened.

Not again. Dammit, not again.

"Come on, Annie. Tell me what's going on. You're white as a ghost."

She wrenched her gaze from the inky, ominous blackness to the man who stood beside her looking ruggedly masculine even with a dishrag in his hand.

She couldn't tell Joe about the photograph. She *couldn't*. He would only worry and fret and use this as an excuse not to take the job opportunity in Wyoming. She refused to do that to him.

Besides, it was only somebody's idea of a stupid, silly prank. It *had* to be. With a deep, calming breath, she forced the fear down so that the cool voice of reason could reassert itself. Just a joke, that's all. What else could it possibly be? Nobody had any reason to frighten her anymore.

That was Charlie's specialty and he was gone—living in New Mexico somewhere, according to his sleazebag of a lawyer. He wouldn't dare show himself around Madison Valley again, not unless he wanted to find himself behind bars.

His good-old-boy network wouldn't be able to protect him anymore. Now that Bill Porter had been voted out of the sheriff's office, Charlie had no more influence with local law enforcement.

John Douglas, the new sheriff, had been the deputy who investigated Charlie's last drunken attack on her— the beating that nearly killed her and finally convinced her that she had to break free, for the children's sake if nothing else.

Douglas had been caring and committed, and she knew he was more than willing to pursue charges if her ex-husband ever showed his face around town again.

She wouldn't be Charlie's victim anymore.

Or anyone else's, for that matter.

"Annie?"

Joe gripped her shoulder to turn her toward him. The heat of his touch forced its way past her nerves—past the fear—and zinged right to her stomach. He stood only a few inches away from her, a tall, lean man, hardened and toughened by life.

With any other man she might have been uneasy at

his closeness, at the leashed power in those thick muscles. But this was Joe.

Joe's arms would give only comfort, a safe haven, and she suddenly wanted them around her with a fierce intensity that alarmed her far more than any noises she heard outside.

Her body instinctively swayed toward him, drawn to his warmth and strength like metal shavings toward a magnet. Instead of pulling her close, though, instead of folding her into the solace of his arms, he dropped his hand from her shoulder as if he'd touched the electric fence around the south pasture.

Cheeks flaming, she backed away from him and returned to the sink to gaze out the window. She could sense him watching her, feel the heat of that black-eyed gaze.

She had always thought Joe would have made a good cop—he could stare the truth out of anybody. But she wouldn't bend this time.

He must have reached the same conclusion. He sighed, a soft, frustrated sound in the quiet kitchen. "You're not going to tell me what's bothering you, are you?"

"There's nothing to tell," she lied. "I'm just edgy from the storm, that's all."

"You could teach stubborn to a blasted mule."

Before she could answer, C.J. came bursting into the kitchen. "Hey Mom! There's gonna be a show on next about panda bears in China. Want to come watch?" His voice trailed off when he saw Joe standing by the mudroom door. Her son's finely drawn features twisted into a frown.

"Why is *he* still here?"

"He helped clean up the kitchen."

"It looks clean to me, so he can leave now." He glared at Joe. "You're good at that, right?"

Great. Now she had two moody, angry children to deal with. She gave C.J. a stern look. "That is quite enough, young man."

"Why are you mad at me? He's the one who's leaving."

"That doesn't give you the right to be rude. Apologize right now and then I think we need to skip the show about pandas tonight. Turn the TV off. You can play in your room for a while before bed."

With another glare toward her this time, C.J. mumbled an apology that was miles away from being sincere, then stormed out of the room before she could call him on it.

Joe shoved his hat on but not before she saw pain and regret flash in his eyes. She wanted to soothe it, to comfort him, but she didn't know where to begin.

"I'm sorry," she finally said. Her apology was at least heartfelt. "I thought he would have begun to accept your new job by now but apparently he still has a ways to go."

Joe shrugged into his coat. "He has a right to be upset."

"But not to vent his feelings by hurting others. I won't tolerate it and he knows it."

Charlie used to say she was going to turn C.J. into a weak little mama's boy with all her talk about politeness and correct behavior. Maybe she was a little demanding, but what choice did she have? Every time her son raised his voice or even *thought* about bullying someone else, she worried he would turn out like his father.

These last months with Joe had been so good for C.J. He had finally had the example of a decent, hardworking man to follow. She hoped Joe had shown him that a man didn't have to be rough and menacing to be masculine, that most of the time quiet strength could get a lot further in life than brawn and bluster.

Who would teach him these things after Joe left? She sighed. Just another thing to worry about.

"He'll get over it eventually, I promise," she said. "Just give him time."

But both of them knew time was something they didn't have the luxury of enjoying anymore. Joe shoved his hat on his head and shrugged into his coat, then turned the conversation back to her edginess. "If you change your mind and need to talk about whatever's bothering you, you know where to find me. Good night, Annie. Sleep tight."

She watched him go out into the cold knowing perfectly well that she wouldn't sleep tight, that she would toss and turn all night, thinking of a wounded little boy and a spooky, voyeuristic Polaroid picture and the man who would be walking out of her life in just a few short weeks.

Chapter 5

"Almost there. Just a few more minutes…got it."
Annie carefully pulled the needle out of the little calf's
side. "Okay, Luke. You can let him out now."

The ranch hand worked the latch on the network of
chutes and the bawling little Hereford darted through
the gate then headed off across the snow-covered winter
range to find his mother.

Annie stood and tried to stretch the kinks out of her
back while Luke grabbed one of the canteens hanging
over the metal chute and took a grateful swig of water.

She knew just how he felt. Immunizing calves could
be sweaty, exhausting work even when the temperatures
were only in the midtwenties. She wasn't about to com-
plain, though. Midtwenties beat below zero anytime in
her book.

The vicious cold front of the week before had finally
headed south, returning temperatures to their seasonal
norms. Even though it was still cold, at least she could

stand to stay outside now for more than a few minutes without feeling as if the air were being squeezed from her lungs by vicious, icy hands.

Here in the pale winter daylight, surrounded by lowing cattle and the sharp, familiar scents of alfalfa hay and manure, the frightening incident with the photograph the week before seemed as far away as the sun.

Just her imagination. That's all it had been. One of the men had played a cruel, senseless prank on her and she had let herself get entirely too carried away by it.

Nothing else out of the ordinary had happened since then. If she sometimes seemed to feel icy fingers glide down her spine with the sensation of someone watching her, well, that too was just her imagination working overtime.

"Hey, quit loafing over here. We got work to do." Manny Santiago rode up to them, his teeth gleaming in the sunlight as a grin split his dark, handsome face.

She pushed the thoughts of that eerie photograph out of her mind and looked up at him, forcing a smile. "Yeah, yeah. Easy for you to say. You've got the best part."

Manny had won the coin toss and drew out the enviable task of rounding up the calves, with the help of the dogs.

"Any time you want to trade, let me know," she went on. "I could use some time on the back of a horse."

"How many more?" Manny asked.

"I don't know. Let me check." Annie picked up the computerized printout, grateful again for technology that helped her easily track each calf through every stage of its life on the Double C.

In the old days, her father would have pages and

pages of data about the herd. Now everything was on computer, from the moment the calf came into the world until he met his inevitable end.

"We're about halfway there," she answered. "About a hundred more. We still might beat the others."

"I hope so, boss. I could really use that twenty bucks."

She sent him a teasing grin. "Quit stalling, then. Get out there and bring us some more calves. I think it's fair to say the other team isn't just going to hand it to us. They all want the prize, too."

Joe had turned the drudgery of vaccinating the new calves into a contest—the first team to take care of its allotted calves would each earn an Andrew Jackson.

He was so good at getting the most out of the men. He always seemed to know exactly what they needed to spur them to work harder and faster. Annie sighed, depressed again at the idea of trying to find someone to replace him.

While she waited for Luke to set up the next calf, she watched Manny go to work, with help from her best cow dog. Dolly's black and white belly brushed the snow as she effortlessly separated another calf from its mother. Together the border collie and the cowboy drove the calf into the overflow chute, without Dolly even having to nip at the animal.

"That sure is one fine dog." Following her gaze, Luke shook his head in admiration.

Annie couldn't agree more. Although Dolly was nearly fourteen, the border collie still could outwork any of the other three dogs on the ranch, all half her age or younger.

Her father had prided himself on the quality of his herders and he used to spend hours training them. As far as Annie was concerned, Dolly was better than any of them had been.

"Should have named her Shadow, though." Luke flashed her a grin just as Annie slid the a needle under the hide of the next bawling calf.

"Why's that?" she asked, only half-listening to him.

"The way she follows you around and all."

Annie smiled as she pulled the needle out. "She always has, I suppose because I trained her from a pup. We've been through a lot together."

Now there was an understatement. Dolly had been one of her best protectors during her marriage. She had hated Charlie fiercely—a sentiment he returned wholeheartedly—and she instinctively seemed to sense when he'd been drinking and was at his most dangerous.

She would always bark like crazy, giving Annie enough advance warning so she could retreat somewhere he wouldn't dare bother her, either her own room or one of the children's.

Ah, the joys of matrimony.

She blew out a breath and forced herself to turn back to the job at hand. "Okay, that one's done. Ninety-nine more."

"Have you given any more thought to hiring me to take over for Joe?" Luke asked suddenly.

At the completely unexpected question, she fumbled with the hypodermic and would have dropped it into the mud they'd churned up through the snow if her instincts hadn't kicked in at the last minute. She ended up catching it in midair.

"What… What did you say?"

"You know. What we talked about the other night. About hiring me to be foreman after Joe leaves."

Dumbfounded, for a moment she could do nothing

but stare at him. She thought she had made it abundantly clear he wasn't even in the running for the foreman position. Good grief. Did he need to be knocked over the head with it?

She sat back on her heels, fumbling for words just like she had just fumbled the syringe. "Luke, I told you I wanted someone with a little more experience," she finally said. "I'm sorry, but I'm not going to change my mind about it."

He didn't seem at all fazed by her answer, just gave her a smile brimming with cockiness. "You will. Just wait."

The complete conviction in his voice astounded her but before she could answer, the muffled thud of horse hooves on snow sounded in the clear, cold air.

Joe rode across the pasture toward them on Quixote, his big bay gelding. He wore jeans, a lined denim jacket, his customary black Stetson and leather gloves—the standard winter attire of all the cowboys who worked the Double C. Manny and Luke deviated only in the color of their hats.

But somehow Joe made the clothes look far different than either of the other men. He seemed so perfectly right on the back of the muscular horse—so wholly, ruggedly male—that her stomach quivered in reaction.

He always made her feel completely feminine by comparison, even when she was grubbing around in the snow and the mud in her ratty old ranch coat and beat-up ropers.

Joe was the kind of man who turned heads wherever he went, just by his sheer physical presence. He always had been. Even as a boy he had been strikingly beautiful, and all the girls at school used to have crushes on him. Joe ignored all of them except for Annie, which didn't exactly win her points with the other girls. Not that she cared much. She hadn't had much patience for other girls her age.

If anything, age and life had only improved Joe's looks, had hardened his sculpted features to masculine perfection. With that exotic copper skin, his piercing dark eyes and that full, sensuous mouth—not to mention the air of barely leashed danger surrounding him in an almost visible aura—it was no wonder women still acted like fluttery idiots around him.

Including her.

Annie jolted back to earth and to the calf bawling in the pen in front of her, suddenly remembering the bet.

"Your team can't be done yet!" she exclaimed. "No way!"

Joe's grin nearly stopped her heart. "Scared, are you?"

She took a deep, fortifying breath, relieved to find her blood still pumping, her lungs still working. "Not at all. We're gonna kick your butts. Aren't we, boys?"

"Hell, yeah." Luke's chest puffed with bravado and Manny's grin flashed in his dark face.

"Right into next week, boss," he said.

Joe rested both hands on the saddle horn as Quixote stamped a few times in the snow and puffed out a cloudy breath, eager for action.

Like most modern ranches, the Double C had a couple of snowmobiles and two four-wheelers but she and Joe both preferred to do things the time-honored way whenever possible. A snowmobile could never take the place of a good cutting horse, and Qui was one of the best she'd ever seen.

She gave the big bay a pat, then turned to Joe with a smirk. "We're especially going to kick your butts if you spend all day checking up on us. Worry about your own calves, why don't you?"

"Well, you know, I'd like to do that but for some reason we didn't have enough needles to finish the job. You wouldn't have shortchanged us on purpose, would you?"

"Why on earth would I do that?"

He shrugged. "Maybe you were trying to sabotage our chances at winning the contest."

You stupid bitch. Can't you do anything right? You're always trying to ruin everything for me.

His words sparked another of those damn flashbacks. It took her completely by surprise. She hadn't had one for months, but for a moment she froze.

Locked in the past, she felt herself respond—felt her head bow, her shoulders hunch in foreboding—and she could think of nothing else but escaping.

Eventually through the old haze of misery and fear, reality intruded. Joe would never hurt her. Her mind knew it even if her instincts had been conditioned to cower.

She looked up and found him watching her with a smile in his eyes. Teasing. He was teasing her.

Calming breaths. Deep, calming breaths. With effort, she made her muscles relax and when the fear finally fled she forced herself to play along, raising a haughty eyebrow as if nothing had happened. "Why would I have to resort to sabotage? We were going to win anyway."

"Just hedging your bets, maybe. Our team mysteriously ran out of sharps halfway through our calves and last I checked, you were the one handing out the supplies."

No wonder she'd been thrown off balance. She

wasn't used to Joe in this teasing mood. Even when he was younger, he'd always been far too serious and his time in prison had only made him more somber.

Apparently the men weren't used to it either. Manny watched the exchange avidly from his saddle and even Luke had dropped what he was doing to lean his elbows on the rail of the chute.

She tried to ignore them both.

"I had nothing to do with it." She gave a small, prim smile, vastly relieved that the flashback hadn't been a bad one. "What I gave you should have been more than enough. You probably dropped them in the snow somewhere."

"That's what I would have suspected too, except you do have a reputation to uphold."

"What are you talking about? I always play fair!"

"Do the words 'letter jacket' mean anything to you?"

The memory surprised a laugh out of her, conjuring up a long-forgotten memory. She'd been about eleven, Joe and Colt fifteen. The three of them had been moving irrigation pipes on the Broken Spur one summer day and Joe had boasted that he could ride any horse on either of their ranches. She had bet him his brand-new football letter jacket that she could find a horse he couldn't ride.

She laughed again, remembering the completely baffled look on his face when he had hit the dirt. "You just can't let it go, can you? Twenty years later and you can't forget."

"You cheated, Annie. You never told me you had a ringer, a wild mustang your dad had just brought to the ranch. It was a dirty trick. Can you blame me for being suspicious now?"

"I gave you back your stupid jacket."

"Only because your dad forced you to."

She grinned at him, relishing their banter. She had a sudden, fierce wish that they could travel back in time to the days when their friendship was pure and uncomplicated. Before the terrible summer when their world had changed forever.

Her smile faded. They couldn't go back, any more than they could change the past. And soon all she would have left of him would be those memories.

She picked up a handful of wrapped needles from the box in front of her and held them out. "Here. Take as many as you need," she said, her voice short. "Want us to take some of your calves to make it fair?"

His own smile slid away and he didn't say anything for a moment, as if sensing her mood. Finally he took the needles from her. "No. Wouldn't want to give you any reason to say we didn't win fair and square."

He wheeled Quixote around, then the horse cantered off across the pasture, leaving her watching after him.

Joe poked at the cedar log in the fireplace, sending sparks fluttering up the chimney. Outside the wood-frame foreman's cottage, snowflakes drifted softly to earth. But inside the four-room cottage was warm and cozy.

He watched the fire for a few moments, lost in the hypnotic dance and sway of the flames and the hiss and chatter of wood being consumed, then he returned to the easy chair facing it.

This is what he had missed so desperately in prison—this satisfying ache in his muscles from knowing he'd put in a good, honest day's work, the calm assurance that he'd left no chores undone, a warm, comfortable chair, and a good book to come home to at the end of the day.

Other inmates filled the endless hours in the joint talking of what they missed most on the outside—their friends or their women or their whiskey. But Joe had dreamed of only simple, pure moments like this.

And of Annie.

He picked up his book, angry at himself for always coming back to her. He'd had no business dreaming of her then and he had even less business dreaming of her now.

Besides, the laughing, gutsy girl that had sustained him through those grim years when he thought he would shatter apart if he had to endure one more day was just a memory. That girl didn't exist anymore.

In her place was a sad-eyed, skittish woman who jumped at shadows and trusted no one.

Occasionally the girl he had known reappeared, though. This afternoon, for instance. He set the book down and gazed once more at the flames as if he could conjure her there.

It had been so good to see Annie laughing and joking with him, to see that flush on her cheeks again and that sassy spark in her eyes.

He missed the old Annie, the one who used to see the world as one big challenge for her to conquer. The Annie who found joy in the simplest of things and who was willing to take on a bully twice her size on the school bus when Joe stoically refused to respond to his taunts.

He hadn't realized how much he missed her until he caught that rare, fleeting glimpse today.

He had loved that girl. It had been his guilty secret through most of his life. Annie had represented everything he didn't have in his life—sweetness, laughter, joy—and he had craved her like an addict desperate for his next fix.

He'd tried to hide it and thought he had succeeded pretty well until the day he had found her grieving for her father up at the lake. He had kissed her only in comfort, but that one embrace had sent all his bottled-up feelings—some he hadn't even admitted to himself—exploding out of him like Roman candles.

The memory was etched in his mind, right alongside the day he learned she had married his brother.

He found out the same day he had been transferred from the county jail to Deer Lodge. He didn't know what he remembered more, his first official day as a convicted murderer or that solemn, devastating letter from Colt.

Annie and Charlie.

He had thought it was a joke at first. When he finally realized Colt was serious, he thought he was suffocating, being buried alive.

She hadn't even bothered to write to him herself. He was amazed at how much that still hurt, even though he admitted he was probably to blame for that. She had tried to come visit him before his sentencing and he wouldn't even see her. He had been too ashamed to let her see him.

Maybe if he hadn't been so stubborn, maybe if he could have swallowed his pride, he might have been able to talk some sense into her before she did something so disastrous as marry his brother.

It was the past, he reminded himself, picking up his book with determination. It was over and done with. Dredging it all up again was pointless—not to mention masochistic.

Despite his best efforts to concentrate on the mystery, he still hadn't turned a single page twenty minutes later when a knock sounded through the cottage.

He sighed and balanced the book on the padded arm of the chair. So much for his quiet night in front of the fire. Trouble was the only thing to come knocking on the foreman's door this late at night.

It was probably Mitchell. At dinner the rest of the men said they were going into Lulu's in town to waste the bonus he'd ended up having to give all of them.

Just his luck that his brainy idea for a vaccination contest would end in a dead tie between both teams— they'd all ridden back to the barn at exactly the same moment. He'd been obligated to fork over eighty bucks, twenty each to the four hands.

He had planned to pay out of his own pocket—it was his idea, after all—but Annie wouldn't let him. She'd insisted on using ranch reserves. The men deserved it, she said, and she only wished she'd thought of it first.

She was a good boss, even though she still didn't have much confidence in herself.

And how could he blame her for that? When she was a child she'd had to deal with her father's harsh expectations and vocal disappointment that she hadn't been a son. Then as an adult she'd had to deal with Charlie.

He put the thought away and swung open the door.

To his surprise, it wasn't Luke standing on his step but Annie, hands shoved into the pockets of a thin jacket and her shoulders bowed against the cold night.

Chapter 6

"What's wrong?" he asked instantly, taking in the worry in her eyes and the lines bracketing her mouth.

"I'm being stupid. Probably nothing. It's just…" She chewed on her lip. "I saw your light on and thought I'd ask. Did you see Dolly by any chance when you were doing the evening feeding?"

He frowned, trying to remember. "No. I think the last time I saw her was this afternoon when we all came back after finishing up the shots. Why? What's the matter?"

"Probably nothing." She blew out a breath. "I just can't find her anywhere. I've looked in all her usual hideouts but she's not in any of them. I don't know where else to look."

As the surprise at finding her knocking on his door this late at night began to wear off, he started to notice other details about her appearance. Huge white flakes of snow stood out in stark relief against the auburn of her hair, her face was pale and set, and her lips had an ominous blue tinge to them.

Didn't the woman have more sense than to wander outside in the middle of the night during a Montana February wearing only a thin jacket? She colored at his scrutiny and reached a hand—a bare hand, he noted with aggravation—and swiped at the snow in her hair.

"Where are your gloves?" he snapped. "What were you thinking to go outside in the middle of the night without a good coat on? Do you want to freeze to death?"

She shoved her hands back into her pockets. "I didn't expect to be out this long. I thought I'd only be going to the barn for a moment, just long enough to find Dolly and take her back to the house for the night."

He wasn't helping the situation at all by forcing her to stand in the open doorway while he yelled at her, he realized. He opened the door wider. "Come inside by the fire. We'll get you warmed up first and then you can tell me why you're so worried about her."

He urged her toward the easy chair by the fireplace, then sat at the ottoman at her feet and enfolded her hands in his much larger ones to warm them with his body heat.

While he rubbed at her icy fingers he tried fiercely not to think about how soft her skin felt beneath his hands or just how his mouth could warm her trembling lips.

He didn't realize he was staring at those lips, picturing his mouth fitting perfectly over hers, until they parted slightly as if on a sigh. He lifted his gaze to hers and found her staring back at him, her eyes huge and color now high in her pale face.

The atmosphere pulsed with sudden tension. He saw

awareness in the widening of her pupils, felt it in the fluttering of her hands in his, and realized with a stunning jolt that she wouldn't stop him if he leaned forward and gave in to the impulse to kiss her.

Her mouth would be soft and cool and would probably taste like apples, just like the rest of her.

He couldn't help himself, he focused on her mouth again, and he saw her breath catch. It was just a tiny hitch, not even a full-fledged gasp, but it was enough to yank him back to his senses.

He jerked back, appalled at himself. Dropping her hands, he shoved the ottoman back so he could stand and tried to focus on her reason for being here instead of all the hundreds of reasons he wanted to kiss her—and the thousands more why he couldn't.

"Tell me why you're so worried about Dolly," he asked abruptly. "She can take care of herself."

She blinked a few times at his curtness and at the rapid mood shift, then that dazed awareness in her eyes changed back to worry for her dog. "She's getting old, Joe. She'll be fourteen this summer. I don't know where she finds the energy to even keep up with the other dogs, let alone work them into the ground like she does."

"She's always been one great cow dog. The kind that could win contests if you ever entered her. You did a real fine job training her."

"I think she trained me more than the other way around." A smile twisted her mouth then faded quickly. "I've started bringing her inside to sleep lately because the cold seems to bother her so much, but she didn't come up to the house tonight like she usually does. I went to look for her and she's not with the rest of the dogs in the big barn."

"What about the hay shed? You know how she likes to sneak in there and make a little nest for herself on the loose hay."

"I thought of that. That's the first place I checked after I went to the barn, but she wasn't there either. She always—*always*—comes when I call, but tonight she didn't. It scares me."

A hundred things—hell, a thousand—could happen to an aging dog on a spread the size of the Double C. She could have fallen through the thin layer of ice at the creek or been caught by a falling hay bale or dropped her guard around one of the cattle and been gored.

Damn. Annie loved that dog. He hated to think of her heartache if the dog was lying hurt somewhere. Or worse.

He headed toward the coatrack by the door for his own winter gear. "I'm sure she's fine but why don't you stay here by the fire and I'll go out and see if I can find her."

Annie stiffened. "Forget it. She's my dog. I'm going with you."

"You're still so cold you're shivering."

The subtle trembling of her shoulders inside her coat brought all his anger flashing back. "What were you thinking, anyway? Even if you were only going out for a moment, a single-layer denim coat is worthless against this kind of cold. You know that. You're not dressed to go running around outside any more tonight, so be sensible for once and stay right here where it's warm and dry."

She shook her head and rose from the easy chair. "I'll hurry over to the house and put on my warmer coat and gloves. It will only take a couple of minutes,

I promise, just the time it will take you to saddle a couple of horses for us.''

He knew that stubborn light in her green eyes only too well. ''You're not going to budge on this, are you?''

''What do you think?''

He sighed. ''That I'd better go saddle a couple of horses.''

His disgruntled tone finally pierced her determination. Too late, she absorbed the particulars of the room, details she'd overlooked in her worry over Dolly—the mystery novel straddling the arm of the chair, the low jazz murmuring from the stereo, the steam curling up from a mug of what looked like hot cocoa.

And he was dressed for relaxing, in soft, faded jeans and a charcoal sweater that made the black of his hair stand out.

How dense could she be? He'd obviously been settling in for a cozy night in front of the fire and here she was filling up what was probably his only time to unwind with more of her problems.

When was she going to learn to take care of her troubles by herself without constantly bothering him with them?

She bit her lip. ''I'm sorry, Joe. I wasn't thinking. I should have realized I was intruding on your time off. Don't worry about Dolly, you don't have to help me. I'll find her—just go back to your book.''

He didn't answer her, just gave her the same ''don't be stupid'' look he used to aim at her when they were younger and she would try to ride home by herself from the Broken Spur in the dark.

''Come on,'' he finally said. ''I'll walk you to the house on the way to the horse barn.''

Reluctantly, she followed him out the door. The snow

still drifted down slowly, big fat flakes that shimmered in the glow from the vapor light on a power pole between the foreman's cottage and what had always been called the big house. The temperatures had dropped into the teens, she figured. He was right, she should have been more sensible and worn her heavier coat.

He shortened his steps to compensate for her much shorter stride and they walked up the drive in silence. After that charged encounter inside his house, she was intensely aware of him, of his dark hair curling slightly over his collar and the determined set of his mouth and the way his shoulders filled the bulky material of his coat.

They were cry-on-me shoulders, as she knew only too well. She was always entirely too quick to take him up on it, to turn to him whenever she had a crisis.

Why was that? she wondered. What was it about Joe that compelled everyone to lean on him?

When she was a girl she was always running to him with every little injustice in her stupid, sheltered life: a poor grade on a school assignment, another child on the playground who pulled her hair, an unkind word from her father.

She cringed now to think of all the times she had gone whining to him. He had always been so calm, wise beyond his years, with an air of quiet, calming strength that she had shamelessly exploited.

It should have been the other way around. He'd had far more to cry about in his life. She had known what it was like at home for him. Maybe not the full extent of it, but she could guess with pretty grim accuracy now, especially after being married to Charlie for ten years.

Charlie had never touched the children, though; she

wouldn't have tolerated it for a second if he had. Albert Redhawk, on the other hand, had been indiscriminate with his cruelty, dispensing it freely to his first and second wives and to the son he had from each.

Joe wouldn't discuss his home life. At least not honestly.

She remembered asking him once when they were riding home together on the bus why his mother never smiled or laughed. She could vividly remember wishing fiercely that she could take the question back when his mouth quivered like he was going to cry.

But he hadn't cried, instead he had made up some silly story about how an evil shaman put a curse on Mary. If she ever smiled again, she would have to give Joe to the bad medicine man, and Mary loved her son far too much for such a horrible fate. Giving up smiles and laughter was a small price to pay to protect her boy.

Annie couldn't have been more than six or seven at the time, so gullible she sincerely believed quarters could grow out of her ears whenever Patch would pluck one out during his sleight-of-hand magic tricks, but even then she had known Joey was lying.

She knew now why Mary Redhawk never smiled. Knew the reasons all too well.

She pushed the thought away. She wasn't a victim like Mary anymore, she was a strong, confident woman.

And maybe if she kept telling herself that, she might eventually believe it.

"It shouldn't take me long to change my coat," she said when they reached the big house a few moments later.

"Don't forget your gloves and a good hat."

She rolled her eyes. "Yes, mother."

"I'll take a look for Dolly in the outbuildings again and then meet you in a few moments at the barn."

She nodded and hurried into the house for her shearling coat and lined ropers. By the time she reached the barn, Joe was throwing a saddle blanket over her big dun mare.

"You didn't see her either?"

Joe shook his head. "Not in any of the obvious places. I guess we'll have to start looking in the unobvious places. You're going to feel pretty silly when we find her curled up somewhere warm, sleeping soundly."

"I hope so. I really hope so."

She watched him work for a moment, as always in awe of the way the horses responded to his quiet murmurs. "I'll get the saddles," she offered after a moment, and opened the door to the little tack room at one end of the horse barn.

Switching on the light, she quickly found her saddle, then started to go back out into the barn when she heard a small rustling sound and the tiniest of whimpers.

She whirled around and searched through the clutter, until her gaze landed on a small quivering mound of black and white fur on top of a pile of saddle blankets.

Dolly! The whisper of sound she'd heard was her tail brushing weakly along the floor.

"Joe! In here!" she yelled, dropping the saddle as she rushed toward the little border collie. Dolly whimpered again in greeting and tried to put her nose in Annie's hand but she didn't have the strength to lift her head off the ground.

Her nose was cold, so cold, and she was trembling violently. She didn't have the strength to even lift her head off the blankets and she looked at Annie through dull, pain-filled eyes.

Joe ran in but stopped in his tracks when he saw the dog. "What's wrong with her?"

"I don't know." She barely spared him a glance as she ran her hands gently over fur, looking for anything that might explain the obvious pain and this awful, awful shaking.

"Anything broken?"

"I don't think so." She frowned. "How did she get in here? The door was latched tight."

"Maybe somebody left it open. She could have wandered in and then the wind blew it shut or something."

"Maybe." Helplessness swamped her and for the life of her, she couldn't think what to do next.

She would have stood there for several more moments but to her relief, Joe stepped forward to take over.

"Let's get her up to the house where it's warm. We can call Doc Thacker from there." With a gentle concern that brought the harsh sting of tears to her eyes, he scooped the dog up into his strong arms and led the way out of the horse barn.

Annie trudged through the snow behind them, her heart aching. She hated to see Dolly in such pain and was terrified the veterinarian would say she would have to be put down.

If that's the course of action Graham recommended, how would she ever find the strength to say goodbye?

A tight knot formed in her stomach while she called the veterinarian's emergency number from the phone in the kitchen, then she quickly returned to the family room.

Joe had placed Dolly on a blanket in front of the woodstove and he knelt beside her, petting her trembling sides and speaking soft, meaningless words of solace. The sight of such a big, hard man being so gentle with an old dog was almost more than she could handle.

She gulped back the tears and saw that he had taken time to throw a log into the woodstove. Heat poured out of it in soothing waves and flames flickered and danced through the glass door. The heat seemed to be working—Dolly's shivers had quieted to a soft trembling now.

"How is she?"

He looked up. "I can't tell. She seems a little better. What did Graham say?"

The local vet, Graham Thacker, lived just a few miles from the Double C, on the other side of the Broken Spur. She shrugged. "He couldn't diagnose her over the phone so he's going to come by and take a look at her. Said it would be easier than having both of us drive into the clinic in town."

"Makes sense."

She folded to her knees beside the little border collie, conscious of Joe's gaze on her.

"How are *you* doing?" he asked softly.

The sting behind her eyes became a full-fledged burning ache. She *wouldn't* break down. She wouldn't. Even if that tender concern in his voice was just about sweetest thing she'd ever heard.

She swallowed hard and looked down at Dolly's head in her lap. "I'll be okay."

He didn't say anything for several moments and the only sound in the room was the dog's soft panting and the crackle and hiss of the fire, then Joe reached out and cupped her shoulder. Just that, the simple comfort of his touch, sent a tear slipping out before she could stop it.

Thank heavens her back was to him and he couldn't

see her being such a blubber baby. He gave her one quick, comforting squeeze, then withdrew his warmth and strength. "I need to go back to the barn to take care of the horses."

He'd been in the middle of putting on their tack and had come running when she found Dolly, she realized. "I completely forgot about them. I'm glad you remembered."

"I'll come back to the house when I'm done, okay?"

She looked up to meet his questioning gaze. He was asking if she wanted his help and she didn't know how to answer. She should be able to handle this by herself. She'd handled much, much worse, hadn't she?

She almost told him to go on home, back to his warm fire and his book and his hot cocoa. The words hovered on her tongue for a few moments but in the end she couldn't bring herself to utter them.

She needed him.

Whether she liked it or not, she just couldn't face the many grim possibilities the vet might offer all by herself.

"Thank you," she murmured again, and forced a smile of gratitude. "You're a good friend, Joe. I don't know what I'd do without you."

An odd, almost bitter expression flashed in his eyes, then he shoved his Stetson back onto his dark hair and headed out into the night.

Chapter 7

By the time Joe finished with the horses and returned to the house, he was relieved to see the vet's pickup already parked in front of the house. Thacker was a good man. He'd be willing to bet there weren't too many veterinarians willing to climb out of a warm bed in the middle of the night to make a house call on an old, ailing dog.

Thacker was also damn good at his job, and Joe figured Annie's dog would be back on her feet before they knew it.

Not wanting to wake the kids, he didn't bother to knock, just let himself in. As soon as he walked through the quiet house to the family room, he knew something was drastically wrong. Thacker wore a worried frown that made his wrinkled face resemble a bulldog even more than it usually did and Annie looked like she'd just taken a fist to the gut.

"What is it?" he asked.

Both of them turned at his voice. Annie spoke first, her voice flat, empty, and in sharp contrast to the stark emotion in her features. "Graham thinks Dolly has been poisoned."

He whipped his gaze from her toward the dog still quivering in front of the fire then to the veterinarian. "Doc, are you sure about this?"

Thacker returned a stethoscope to the big leather bag he always carried. "Can't be a hundred percent. Not without blood tests. But that's what my gut is telling me. "

"What makes you even suspect that?"

"Once you've seen a dog with metaldehyde poisoning, you don't easily forget it. She's got classic symptoms. The convulsions are the real giveaway."

"Metaldehyde?" Joe asked.

"Slug bait. I've seen a few other cases through the years, but it's not something we run into too often. We don't have much of a slug problem around here so it's not a poison people generally leave lying around for their pets to get into. You wouldn't happen to have used some this year, have you?"

Annie shook her head. "I have plenty of aphids in my garden but never slugs. Anyway, all the fertilizers and insecticides we use on the ranch are locked up in one of the sheds. She couldn't possibly get to them."

"So you think somebody did this on purpose?" Joe asked.

The vet's bushy gray eyebrows drew together when he frowned. "I don't know what else to think. But I'd bet my practice that when I run the blood sample, we'll find slug bait in her system."

Annie looked near tears as she gazed at the little collie. " Why? Why would somebody do this?"

The vet frowned again. "You tell me."

Annie's eyes were wide and frightened when she raised her gaze. "I have no idea," she said, but then her eyes drifted away. For some reason Joe had the distinct impression she was lying.

Before he could puzzle it out, the vet spoke again. "In most cases like this, it turns out to be an angry neighbor or relative. You made anybody mad lately? Anything else strange been happening around here?"

Annie's eyes darkened to the color of pine needles and she opened her mouth as if she wanted to say something, then she snapped it shut again and shook her head.

Joe could easily read her thoughts in her expression. She would be trying to figure out who would hate her enough to do this and she would probably be blaming herself.

Hadn't she been through enough? Who was vicious enough to lash out at her by using an innocent animal?

Charlie.

He hissed in a breath. No. No damn way. Not that he didn't think his half brother was capable of it—hell, he knew better than most that Charlie was capable of just about anything—but it couldn't be him. Charlie was gone and he wouldn't dare come back.

Joe had done his best to make damn sure of that.

His brother knew that if he ever set foot on the Double C, he would find himself in one of two places, depending on who got to him first, Joe or the sheriff.

If he tangled with the law first, he would end up behind bars for a long, long time after his last vicious attack on Annie left her with two broken ribs and a broken arm that still bothered her when it rained.

And Joe had left his big brother with absolutely no

doubt that if *he* found him first, Charlie would end up right where he belonged.

In hell.

No, Charlie wouldn't be coming back. Either the vet was mistaken about Dolly being poisoned or someone else had done it.

"So what do we do for her now?" Annie asked from her position on the floor.

"She should be out of it most of the night. Just watch her closely. If there's any change in her condition— anything at all—give me a buzz. I'll stop by first thing in the morning to see how she is."

"Do you think I should call the police?"

Graham snapped his bag shut. "Might not hurt to give Sheriff Douglas a heads-up. But I'll warn you now, nonfatal dog poisonings probably won't be a real big priority with him. Especially when we don't have any proof a crime actually occurred."

Joe showed Graham out of the family room. "So what's the prognosis?" he asked quietly once they were out of Annie's hearing. "Do you really think she'll make it, or were you just saying that for her benefit?"

"I think she'll be okay. It's lucky you found her when you did before she went into full-fledged seizures. I'll keep her snookered for a couple days until the toxin works its way out of her system but I don't anticipate any lasting effects."

"And you're sure it's slug bait?"

Graham nodded regretfully. "I wish I could say it was something else, something that just imitates all the symptoms. Maybe I'll find something else when I run the tests, but I doubt it. I hate the idea that somebody might have done this to her on purpose."

He shrugged into his coat. "Of course, there's always

a possibility she found a stash somewhere on one of the neighbors' places, but I really doubt it. Like I said, it's pretty rare around here.''

After Joe said goodbye to the vet, he returned to the family room to find Annie in the same position, hovering protectively over the sedated animal. She looked up when he came into the room and he frowned when he saw how pale and frightened she looked.

Still, she forced a smile. ''I really appreciate all the help you've given me.'' Her voice had clear dismissal in it. ''I think I have everything under control now so you can go on back to the cottage and get some sleep.''

He crossed his arms across his chest. ''Save it, Annie. I'm not going anywhere.''

''You need some rest.''

''And you don't?''

That soft cupid's bow of a mouth tightened. ''Go home, Joe.''

''I'm staying. We can take turns. One of us can watch over her while the other one sleeps.''

''You don't have to do that. I can take care of her.''

He started to argue, then he saw the defeated exhaustion in the droop of her shoulders and the fine lines bracketing her mouth, and he decided to take another route.

''I want to help,'' he answered. ''If you won't accept it for yourself, at least take it for Dolly. You're not going to do her any good if you're completely worn out.''

''You've done enough. You already gave up your whole evening to help me and I want you to know I sincerely appreciate it. But I can't keep turning to you every time something goes wrong in my life.''

He would give anything he had to fix things so nothing else ever went wrong in her life. Since he didn't have that kind of power—and she wouldn't have let him use it, even if he had—he focused on what he *could* do.

"Not every time," he agreed quietly. "Just tonight."

She opened her mouth, probably gearing up for more arguments, but whatever she planned to say was lost amid a giant yawn she tried unsuccessfully to hide.

Joe pressed his point. "You're exhausted and even though you might want to, you just can't stay up all night with her. It wouldn't be good for either one of you. Besides, Dolly's completely out of it. She won't be waking up any time soon and she won't even know either one of us is here."

He pointed toward the couch. "I'll take the first watch. Why don't you stretch out and try to get some rest?"

"I couldn't possibly sleep."

"Try. For me. "

She sent him a sidelong look and he could tell she was wondering how hard he would fight her on this, then she sighed. "I'll lie down because I know you'll hound me about it all night if I don't. But I can tell you right now, I'm not going to nod off."

Ten minutes later, she was as out of it as Dolly. He watched her for a long time, the rise and fall of her chest and the way her lips parted slightly with every breath she took.

She looked delicate, ethereal, with milky-white skin and her fine-boned features, and he wished again that things might have turned out differently between them.

If only he hadn't run away from her all those years ago. If only he had stayed and fought for what he didn't even dare admit to himself he wanted instead of letting all the vast differences he saw between them chase him away.

Now it was too late. Much, much too late.

He knew he had nothing to offer her back then—she was the heiress to a vast, wealthy cattle ranch and he was the son of a drunk bully who was only able to support the family he menaced by the skin of his teeth and the benevolence of his employer.

And what had changed in the past thirteen years? Now she was the *owner* of that cattle ranch and he was the owner of a prison record and precious little else, other than a pickup truck he still had fourteen payments on.

By necessity, he had put his feelings for her away when he came back to Madison Valley, had shoved them way down deep in the recesses of his heart. What else could he do? She had married his brother—his *brother,* of all people—and had given birth to two children.

But sometimes his feelings emerged. Sometimes they bubbled up like boiling water, until they were a hot, heavy ache in his chest. Guilt and love and betrayal all wrapped up in one messy package.

He rubbed at the ache, willing it to subside. Annie could never be his. And if it took moving six hundred miles away to get that through his thick skull, that's what he would have to do.

She awoke an hour before dawn.

Disoriented, she blinked a few times, trying to figure out why she would have been stupid enough to fall asleep on the couch again instead of in her own comfortable bed upstairs.

Her neck had a nasty kink and the room was cold.

She twisted her neck back and forth trying to ease the tightness, then looked toward the woodstove to check the status of the fire.

The sight she found there brought all the events of the previous night rushing back. Joe was sprawled out in the recliner, eyes closed and one hand on the fur of Dolly's back.

He probably dozed off petting her, she thought with a small, tender smile.

The crisis seemed to be over. Dolly slept peacefully, her breathing deep and even. To reassure herself, Annie crossed the room and knelt beside the little collie, moving as slowly and quietly as she could so she didn't wake either the man or the dog.

She ran a quiet hand over Dolly's fur. The dog snuffled in her sleep but didn't awaken. All seemed to be fine, as far as she could tell. Dolly's sides expanded and contracted evenly with each breath, with no sign at all of convulsions.

Annie whispered a prayer of gratitude, fighting the urge to bury her face in Dolly's fur. What would she have done if they hadn't found her in time? If she hadn't gone into the tack room or if Joe hadn't been there to keep her calm or if Graham hadn't been able to come so quickly to sedate her and lessen the seizure's effects?

Annie didn't even want to think about it. She knew Dolly wouldn't be around forever but she couldn't bear the idea that the dog had suffered—and might have died—because of such a vicious, unconscionable act.

Poison.

She shivered at the thought. Graham had to be wrong. He *had* to be. Who would possibly want to poison an innocent dog? What could anyone hope to gain?

It was exactly the kind of thing Charlie would have

done to teach her one of his innumerable lessons. But Charlie was gone, so it had to be someone else. Maybe the same person who had taken that photograph and slipped it under her door.

Dolly's poisoning forced her to rethink her conclusion that the photo was an isolated event, a prank. A chill climbed up her spine again. Were the two incidents related? She couldn't ignore the possibility, not now.

But what could anybody hope to gain, other then terrorizing her? It was a sobering thought, that she might have enemies somewhere out there she wasn't even aware of.

Joe made a low noise in his sleep and she shifted her gaze to him, welcoming the diversion from the ugliness of her thoughts.

He looked so different in sleep, more like the quiet boy she had loved as a child than the hard, forbidding man he had become.

He had taken off his boots some time in the night and he looked strangely vulnerable in his thick wool socks. The right one had a little hole in the toe and she wished she could think of some way to offer to fix it without offending him.

She didn't have the chance to watch him in this kind of unguarded moment very often. After a furtive glance under her eyelashes to make sure he still slept soundly, she decided to allow herself this one harmless indulgence.

And it was definitely an indulgence. Like eating a whole box of chocolates by herself or taking Rio up the High Lonesome trail on a summer day just for the sheer joy of it.

This, though. This was worlds better than any of her other guilty pleasures. Joe was raw, masculine beauty, all chiseled features and hard-hewn man, and she loved looking at him.

She wasn't going to have many more opportunities like this. The days seemed to be slipping away from her—he would be taking his new job in less than five weeks now.

It wasn't like she would never see him again—she could comfort herself with that—but at the same time she knew that any encounters would be sporadic and painfully brief.

Her stomach trembled whenever she thought about how gray and colorless her days would be without him. He would leave a huge, jagged tear in the fabric of her life.

Joe had been part of her existence as long as she could remember. Most of her best memories were tied up with him—riding fence together, dry-fly fishing the Madison, listening to him recite the stories of his people he learned from his mother.

She wanted him to share those stories with her children. Rubbing at her stomach as if she could take away the ache there, she sighed softly. It was only a quiet sound but it was enough to wake him. He had always been a fitful sleeper and his time in prison had only heightened that. Now he went from sleep to consciousness instantly, his long dark eyelashes opening without so much as a flutter.

He gazed at her then at the dog, then muttered an uncharacteristically pungent oath. "I must have fallen asleep."

She hid a smile at the self-condemnation in his tone. "Looks that way."

"Is Dolly all right?" He whispered so he didn't disturb the dog.

"Sleeping soundly," she whispered back. "Graham's treatment seems to have worked."

He raked a hand through his thick, dark hair. "I'm sorry, Annie. I was supposed to be watching her, not snoozing away."

She arched an eyebrow at him. "You were *supposed* to wake me up so I could take a turn at nurse duty instead of trying to stay up all night by yourself."

"I didn't have the heart to wake you. Not when you were snoring away so enthusiastically."

Her heart flip-flopped in her chest at the familiar teasing grin she rarely saw anymore. Sweet Lord, she had missed it, so much that she didn't even mind the old jibe. He and Colt always used to try to convince her she made enough noise to wake the dead.

"I do not snore," she said primly.

His gaze shifted to her pursed mouth, then caught there. To her shock, a strange, murky look suddenly gleamed in his eyes. If that same look had appeared in C.J.'s gaze, she would have kept one eye on the cookie jar and the other on his itchy fingers.

Why would Joe be looking at her as if she possessed something he had suddenly developed a powerful craving to have?

He swallowed hard, a muscle flexing in his jaw, and it took her a few stupid moments to clue in.

He was looking at her as if he wanted to kiss her!

Now it was her turn to swallow, and for the life of her she couldn't figure out how to respond. She was probably misreading things anyway. Joe could hardly stand to touch her most of the time.

Thorny disappointment bloomed in her stomach when he cleared his throat and shifted his gaze away from her toward the window, where dawn began to climb over the mountains dressed in pale rose.

"Guess I'd better head back to the house so I can catch a shower before tackling the morning chores."

She looked down at her hands. "I need to be getting the kids up for school in a few moments or they'll miss the bus."

He tugged his boots on, then stood to leave. She held a hand to stop him before he walked out of the room, needing to say so many things but knowing she could only focus on one of them. "Joe, I...thank you," she said softly.

He shifted uncomfortably. "For what?"

"Everything. For being so willing to go out in the cold to help me search for Dolly last night. For taking care of everything when I was too upset to think straight. For staying even when I told you I didn't need you to."

"It was nothing."

"Not to me." She smiled up at him and once more his gaze caught on her mouth. Instantly the mood shifted back to that strange tension of a few moments before.

"Dammit, Annie," he growled. "Don't look at me like that."

She blinked. "Like what?"

"Like you're wondering what it would be like if I kissed you."

Heat soaked her cheeks. He started it! He was the one who had been staring at her mouth like it was a triple-decker strawberry ice cream cone he couldn't wait to dip into. She would have kept all her wonderings to herself if not for that.

"You're crazy," she lied. "I wasn't thinking anything of the sort."

"Yeah? Well, I was."

He growled something that sounded like "God help me" and then he leaned slowly, adamantly forward.

Chapter 8

He couldn't be about to kiss her. She must have misheard him. Joe always acted about as remote and uninterested around her as if she had no more appeal to him than one of her horned Herefords. It simply wasn't possible!

But she couldn't argue with the dip of his dark head or the subtle sway of his body toward her. She had time only for a quick, shocked intake of breath, for a hard kick of her heart, and then his mouth was on hers.

She spent just an instant trying to puzzle out why he would be kissing her, what she had done to deserve this incredible, unexpected gift, then she was lost to the wonder of it.

It was the perfect kind of kiss: not too hard, not too soft but in some heavenly place in between.

In the nearly fourteen years since the first—and only—time he had kissed her like this, she had forgotten nothing. Not the glide of his mouth against hers or the

warmth of his breath or the sheer emotional onslaught
of his touch.

All of it was imprinted on her synapses, burned into
her memory. To have him kissing her again, to be in
his arms once more like this, seemed like some kind of
miracle. Like one of those surreal, heavenly dreams
adorned with hearts and flowers, where everyone smiled
and treated each other with kindness.

The kind of dreams she never wanted to wake from.

The kiss was gentle—slow and thorough and
lovely—and she wanted to cry from the beauty of it.

She had no idea how long they stood there in the
middle of her family room floor. It could have been a
few seconds or several moments. She completely lost
track of time, mindless to the furnace whooshing to life,
to the tired creaking of the old house, to Dolly's soft,
even breathing.

To everything but Joe's mouth, his touch, his heat.

He made a sound against her lips—it might have been
her name, she couldn't be sure—then he tangled his
fingers in her hair and started to deepen the kiss.

She parted her lips, welcoming him, just as a small
squeak of floorboard upstairs rang through the room like
a foghorn. At the sound, Joe's mouth froze on hers and
he drew in a ragged breath.

Don't stop. Please don't stop.

But she knew he would. Even before she opened her
eyes, she knew he would.

Her gaze met his and she watched the hazy blur of
desire in those black depths shift abruptly to shock and
dismay.

With another ragged breath, he stepped away from
her and the room suddenly felt impossibly cold.

"I've got to…I should…"

He shoved his hands into the back pockets of his old, soft jeans. ''I need to go.''

She nodded. She couldn't think straight right now with all her emotions a huge, overwhelming jumble.

For thirteen years she had been careful to keep her feelings to herself. He hadn't wanted her love; she had known that even as she had given herself to him so many years ago.

He cared about her, she knew that and he had certainly wanted her, at least that day. Maybe he even loved her a little in his own way. But like the red-tailed hawk, Joe soared the air currents of his life in solitude. He always had, even when he was a small boy, and she knew nothing she did would ever change that.

He might have given his friendship to her and to Colt but there was always a part of himself he kept separate from them, a part he would not allow them to touch. Maybe the part his father had scarred forever with his cruel words and his even more cruel fists.

But he was the one who had stepped forward, who had said he wondered what it would be like to kiss her and then had acted on that, and she didn't know what to think about it.

She didn't have time to wonder. The footsteps moved to the stairs and before Joe could put on his coat and Stetson, C.J. padded into the room, his pajamas wrinkled from sleep and his dark hair sticking out every which way. He looked completely adorable, in the way only a sleepy-eyed little boy can manage.

He hadn't come far in the room before he caught sight of Joe and immediately stopped in his tracks. ''What is he doing here again?''

Annie frowned at his belligerent tone of voice.

"We've talked about this," she answered sternly. "Your uncle is welcome here any time he wants."

C.J. glared back at both of them. She met him glare for glare, not willing to tolerate rudeness from him even though she knew it stemmed from pain. Her son lowered his eyes first and his gaze landed on the blanket-covered dog lying as still as death beside the wood-stove.

"What's the matter with Dolly?"

She didn't want to frighten him by telling him Dolly might have been poisoned. He had seen more than enough ugliness in his young life and he certainly didn't need to be exposed to more, especially when she could hardly believe Dr. Thacker's suspicions herself.

She cleared her throat. "She's sick. That's why Joe was here, he helped me with her after the veterinarian came last night."

Fear widened his eyes. "Is she going to—"

"She'll be fine." Joe stepped forward and laid a hand on the boy's shoulder. To Annie's surprise and relief, C.J. didn't shrug off the comforting touch.

Maybe he might be able to find it in his heart to forgive his uncle's desertion after all. She dearly hoped so. These last eighteen months had been wonderful for C.J., finally having a decent, caring male in his life. She would hate for Joe's chance at a new life to cost him the little boy's love.

"She'll be just fine," Joe repeated. "Doc Thacker is the best vet around and he and your mom will take good care of her. Matter of fact, your mom's got a lot to do. Maybe you could help her and the doc out. Sort of be the veterinarian's assistant."

C.J. narrowed his gaze at Joe, intrigued but wary. "How?"

"When you're sick, it can be real real nice for someone to sit beside you and talk to you in a low, soothing voice. Maybe tell you stories or sing you songs."

Her heart squeezed painfully in her chest at his words. Had anyone ever done such a thing for Joe, even when he was a little boy? She seriously doubted it. Albert Redhawk would have considered such tender concern coddling, something he wouldn't have tolerated toward his boys.

"My mom does that when I'm sick." C.J. blurted out the words, then blushed as if afraid it might not be manly to admit it.

Joe shifted his dark eyes from her son to Annie, the expression on his face unreadable. "You're a lucky kid to have such a good mom," he said in a low voice, still looking at her.

After a few beats, he turned back to C.J. "You think you could do that with Dolly when you come home from school?"

C.J. didn't even take time to answer, just dropped immediately to the oatmeal-colored carpet next to the dog. Dolly opened her eyes and weakly brushed her tail against the floor, then rubbed her head against the leg of C.J.'s pajamas.

A smile caught her mouth when her little boy laid a comforting hand on the dog's side. He then proceeded to recite his favorite story—*The Tin Soldier*—in a quiet, soothing voice.

He was a good boy. She had screwed up a lot of things in her life but at least she had done this right. Despite the occasional problems—like Leah's recent run of bad grades and bad attitude—both of her children were sweet and caring at heart.

Things could have been, much, much different. If she

hadn't finally summoned the strength and will to escape from Charlie, she cringed to think how they might have turned out.

She glanced at Joe and found him watching the boy and the dog, tenderness softening his normally remote features. Her smile widened. He was so good with both of the children, always treating them with patience and respect even when they didn't deserve it.

He would have been a wonderful father.

The thought slithered into her mind and she drew in a quick breath, pushing away the familiar prick of guilt. She had wanted to tell him, had wanted desperately to let him know he had left her with more than just a broken heart that day on the banks of Butterfly Lake. She had never had the chance.

If she hadn't been so stupid and naive, she might have found a way. Things might have been so very different. But before she could explore her options, before she could gather the courage to find him and let him know about the child she carried, Joe ended up in jail for killing his father and she had ended up his brother's wife.

"You should have told me," Joe said suddenly. For one terrified second, she thought he had guessed the truth.

"T...told you?"

"That we had our own qualified veterinarian already on staff." He grinned at C.J. "Why have we been paying Doc Thacker so much when C.J. here obviously could have done the job?"

The boy snickered. "I'm not a veterinarian."

"No? Well, you seem to be giving that little border collie just the help she needs."

Through her sudden angst, Annie forced a smile of

agreement. The dog's tail-wagging *did* seem to be a little stronger and she had even found the energy to stick out her tongue so she could lick his hand.

"Can I stay home from school and take care of her? She likes it when I tell her stories."

She gave Joe a "now look what you've started" look and shook her head. "You have a spelling test today you can't miss, honey. I'll watch her while you're in school, I promise. As soon as you come home you can take over. Deal?"

C.J. nodded happily, just as Joe shoved on his Stetson. "You want to tell her a story, too?" he asked, with more enthusiasm toward his uncle than he'd shown since the day he announced he was leaving. "You could tell her a story. I bet she'd like that."

"Maybe later. Right now I have to get out and feed some cattle or they're gonna start eating the fences."

With one last long, searching look at Annie that told her he was thinking of that brief, stolen kiss they had shared, he shoved on his Stetson and walked out of the house.

He just couldn't forget.

Joe thrust the pitchfork into another bale of hay and twisted it apart with quick, hard movements while the cattle milling around the wagon bawled with hunger.

The late February cold seared his throat and his lungs but left his thoughts as clear as the icy day. And as always, they went back to that morning a week earlier when he had made the huge—no, gargantuan—mistake of kissing Annie.

To his immense chagrin, he hadn't been able to think of another damn thing since then. Didn't matter what he was doing, his thoughts would inevitably travel back to that incredible mistake of a kiss.

He'd even taken to eating all his meals at his own place just so he didn't have to watch her mouth curve around a fork and remember just how those lips had felt beneath his.

He was pathetic. Absolutely pathetic.

What in hell possessed him to kiss her like that? he asked himself for at least the thousandth time. One moment he'd been standing in her family room, minding his own business, the next he'd completely lost it and hadn't been able to stop himself from reaching her.

What had he been thinking? Hours after reminding himself of all the reasons they couldn't be together, he practically jumps her.

Well, not quite. He had at least had the sensibility to bite down hard on the need that had exploded to life inside him when she looked at him with want in her big green eyes. But his control had been slipping fast. If C.J. hadn't come down the stairs and interrupted them, he probably would have lost it completely.

Since their kiss, things had been awkward between him and Annie, to say the least. She acted about as skittish around him as a bunch of cows around a family of skunks.

At least C.J. seemed to have forgiven him. The kid had once again taken to following him around every day after school. He didn't know if he felt better or worse to have C.J. talking to him again. It was almost easier when he was still mad; then Joe could let himself forget how much he was going to miss the little rascal.

Miss all of them.

With more force than strictly necessary, he forked the

last alfalfa bale apart for the cattle then climbed back onto the tractor and headed toward the barn.

The ranch seemed strangely quiet when he reached it. No dogs came running out to bark at him as the tractor rumbled in and nothing moved in the cold air but a couple of magpies fighting over something they'd probably scavenged out of the garbage.

He was just starting to get a weird itch between his shoulder blades when Patch stepped out of the barn. The cowboy sent him a friendly wave as Joe stepped down from the tractor.

"Where is everybody?" he asked.

Patch shrugged. "We were running low on vitamins so Miz Annie sent Ruben and Manny into the feed store in town for more. They ought to be back any time now."

"What about Mitchell?"

"He went with the boss gal to ride the fence line between here and the Broken Spur."

Joe frowned at that bit of information. "We just checked that line three days ago. Why is she checking it again?"

"She got a call from McKendrick an hour or so ago. Said a couple of his men saw some Double C stock up by the lake yesterday."

"The lake? Butterfly?"

Patch nodded. "That's what the man said."

They had spent more time rounding up strays these past few weeks than he ever remembered having to do.

Sometimes he could swear the blasted cattle were re-incarnated escape artists, the way they could find the tiniest holes to sneak through. And the ranch did seem to be having more than its fair share of fence trouble this winter.

"I guess we can kiss those cattle goodbye until the snow melts."

"Not if the boss has anything to say about it. She was worried they would starve to death up there."

"There's no way she's going to get up the High Lonesome trail with this much snow."

"Never say never to that gal. You ought to know better than that."

"Why didn't you go with them?"

Patch spat a wad of chew on the ground. "Annie won't let me ride until next week. She's been talking to the doc again."

His hip must be bothering him again, Joe realized with a guilty pang. It was the only reason Annie would have made the old cowboy stay behind while they looked for strays.

He should have been paying more attention. Maggie—Colt's physician wife who had a family practice in Ennis—wanted the old cowboy to see a specialist about a hip replacement. But he was being as stubborn as a one-eyed donkey about it.

Joe should have noticed. It was his *job* to notice. Maybe if he hadn't been so damn distracted by that fateful kiss the other day he might have seen something besides his own problems.

"You need to listen to her," he said now.

"Which one? Annie or the doc?"

"Both of them. You know they're both just trying to look out for you. They both care about you and just want to help."

Patch spat again. "Let me give you a little advice, son. Don't go gettin' old. And if you do, try not to do it around a couple of busybodies like those two."

Joe laughed, but before he could answer, Annie's collie came trotting around the side of the barn. She gave two short barks in greeting, her tail wagging happily.

''Where have you been?'' Joe asked. ''Up to more trouble?''

The dog barked again as if agreeing with him and Joe smiled, happy to see her this energetic. Dolly was almost completely recovered from her slug bait ordeal but she still tired easily and spent much of her time indoors.

Now she sidled up to Patch flirtatiously and nuzzled the old cowboy's leg. Patch patted her head absently. ''Miz Annie won't let you go along either, will she, girl? We both have to stay here together like a couple of lumps and do nothing all day.''

''You can keep each other company.''

Patch rolled his eyes at that, then gave the dog another pat. ''Any news from the sheriff about who might have given her that slug bait?''

Joe shook his head. The day after the poisoning, they found a half-eaten package of doctored hamburger inside the tack room. Given that evidence, Annie had gone to the sheriff but so far John Douglas had no leads. The whole thing scared him to death.

''Fella ought to be strung up,'' Patch muttered darkly. ''Who'd want to do such a thing?''

''I don't know,'' Joe answered. He didn't want to think about it. Between worrying over the dog and stressing over that kiss, he hadn't slept much the last week.

''If you ask me, which nobody ever does, it sounds like just the sort of thing her sumbitch of an ex-husband might have done.''

The old cowboy suddenly flushed crimson above his white handlebar, slow to the realization that Annie's sumbitch ex-husband just happened to be the foreman's brother. "Sorry."

Joe sighed. Did Patch really think he cared what anyone had to say about his brother? "You won't find me defending Charlie to you or to anyone else, Patch. You ought to know that by now."

"I suppose not. Hard to even remember sometimes the two of you are blood."

Not to him. He remembered it every damn time he looked at Annie and thought about kissing her, touching her. He had no right. Not when he was just another no-good Redhawk.

"Guess I'd better get going. The kids will be home from school soon. Wouldn't like 'em to come back to an empty house."

Another pang of guilt hit him while he watched the old cowboy carefully hobble toward the house. It was his job to watch out for his men and he had been so preoccupied with his own life that he'd completely missed the signs that Patch's hip was acting up again.

Annie always saw things like that. What she went through with Charlie would have made many women more self-absorbed, more protective of their own feelings. But not Annie. She showed as much compassion and empathy as she always had.

Maybe even more. Even with running a big operation like the Double C, with all the headaches and stress that entailed, she still found time to watch out for those around her.

She'd always been that way, even when she was a little girl. She had always had this sweet, giving spirit that drew people to her.

When he was a kid and things were particularly bad

at home, he used to be lured toward her like she was the only calm port in a world fierce with storms.

Sometimes in the middle of the night whenever Al was on a rampage or he was hurting too bad to sleep, Joe would climb out the window and take off on one of the Broken Spur horses. He wouldn't even bother to saddle it, would just ride the mile and a half between the two ranches, not sure why he was doing it, just knowing he had to.

He would ride as far as the edge of the south pasture, then walk up the rest of the way and sit propped against the tree outside her window, his spirit calmed in some way he couldn't explain just by knowing she was near.

Sometimes he would even sleep there, with the chirp of crickets to lull him and the warm night air surrounding him like a blanket. But he would always awake in time to ride back to the Double C before anyone figured out he was gone.

The memory made him flush. What kind of stupid kid rides out in the middle of the night just to sit and gaze up at a girl's window?

She would have completely freaked out if she'd known. No, he amended the thought. Maybe her dad would have, since he'd made no secret of the fact he disapproved of any friendship between his daughter and a big, dumb Shoshone, but not Annie.

If she had known about his midnight visits, she would have welcomed him inside, would have held him close and wept silent tears for him. And she would have tried her damnedest to do everything she could think of to make him feel better.

But he hadn't let her. He couldn't let her.

He gave a mental shake to push away the memory. He had work to do, work that wasn't getting done while he stood here rehashing a past that couldn't be changed. He turned to go back into the barn when the low growl of an engine sounded in the clear, cold air.

He glanced toward the sound and thought he saw a flash of silver in the trees about a quarter-mile up the mountain, just at the mouth of the High Lonesome trail.

Damn snowmobilers. He frowned. The mystery of the wandering cattle suddenly became not so curious at all. They spent half the winter replacing fences knocked down by snowmobilers who wandered off national forest land onto the Double C.

Most of them were responsible and truly didn't realize they were on private property, but a small percentage ignored No Trespassing signs, determined to go anywhere they felt they had a right to go and plenty of places they didn't.

Someone who wanted to cause trouble on the Double C could easily access the house by snowmobile.

The thought set him back on his heels. Why hadn't he thought of that before? One of the most puzzling things about Dolly's poisoning was how someone had accessed the ranch without anybody seeing a strange vehicle from the road.

But if somebody rode a snowmobile in and left it on the other side of the creek to hide the telltale engine sounds, he could have walked the rest of the way to the barn, done whatever mischief he set his mind to, then rode away without anybody being the wiser.

Even if somebody saw the tracks in the snow, they wouldn't be suspicious, would just assume the tracks were made by one of the Double C snowmobiles.

That mysterious snowmobiler was probably just somebody out for a pleasure ride. But he didn't like the fact that it was heading toward the same area where Annie and the boy were hunting strays.

He would just check it out. If nothing else, he could help the two of them bring down the stray cattle and make sure Luke Mitchell didn't fall off the mountainside in the process.

Chapter 9

"That's it. That's it. Almost there. Darn!"

As the loop of the lariat landed with a splash in the icy water yet again, Annie blew out a frustrated breath. At the end of her patience, she held a hand out for the rope Luke was ineptly trying to swing. "Why don't you let me have a go at it?"

Luke held tight to the rope, exactly like C.J. used to do when she was trying to help him tie his shoes. "I can do it," he muttered. "I just need a minute."

While you're here monkeying around, the cow is going to drown or freeze to death out there. She clamped her teeth against the words, knowing they wouldn't accomplish anything but hurt a young man's pride.

A low, frightened cry bounced off the snow-covered pine trees as the Hereford struggling to keep her head above water in the frigid, ice-choked depths of tiny Butterfly Lake. Her calf—the same one Annie had delivered the month before, if she wasn't mistaken—bawled piteously in answer from the shoreline.

Poor little cow. They'd come upon her five minutes ago, already weak and terrified as she tried to escape her grim, icy fate.

She must have wandered out onto the frozen lake after making her escape through the broken fence, Annie guessed, although for the life of her she couldn't figure out what might have compelled the stupid animal to do such a thing, especially considering there wasn't a single thing edible for a mile in either direction.

Annie had no idea how long the cow had been out there but she could see the animal's efforts to escape becoming more frantic with every passing second. If they didn't hurry, they would lose her.

With agonizingly slow movements, Luke twirled the rope above his head again. She waited, breath held and nerves twitching, while he let the loop out bigger and bigger, then finally threw it.

It hooked one of the cow's horns this time and she thought it might go all the way over her head. But at the last moment it slipped free, taking the rest of Annie's patience with it.

She held out her hand again. "Okay. My turn."

"I can do it," Luke said testily.

"Give me the damn rope," she growled, past caring about his pride.

Luke set his jaw obstinately and she was afraid for a minute she would have to wrestle it away from him, but he finally surrendered it.

She gripped the lariat in her gloved hand. Now what was she supposed to do? She didn't know if she was any better than Luke with a rope, but she refused to stand here twiddling her thumbs while she watched an animal of hers die.

She had a fierce wish that Joe and Colt were there to help. Joe had an uncanny knack for calming even the most fractious of animals and Colt could rope anything that moved. Between the two of them, they would have had the cow out in moments.

But they weren't there. She was. She owned the Double C and she was responsible for everything on it. She couldn't go on using them as her crutch anymore, especially not with Joe leaving.

If she could do this, could achieve what seemed like the impossible, she could do anything. The seductive thought whispered into her mind and she straightened. She could finally prove to herself she was capable of even the most challenging of tasks.

The floundering cow suddenly took on much more significance. Rescuing her suddenly seemed to represent everything about ranch life she found so difficult.

She gazed out at the thrashing cow, beginning to tire now amid the huge chunks of ice all around. She could get her out. She *would,* even if it killed her.

Just a figure of speech, she assured herself. *Nobody needs to get hurt here.* Not if she was careful.

She would have a better chance of roping the cow if she were closer to her. Thinking quickly, she raced to Rio and pulled the big gelding over to the shoreline, then tied one end of the rope to the horse's saddle horn before heading back toward the shore.

"What are you doing?" Luke asked, his voice shocked, when she didn't stop at the edge of the ice.

She was too busy testing the strength of the ice to pay him any attention. "I'm going out there. I'll have a better chance of roping her if I'm not so far away."

"No way!"

At his panicked vehemence, she glanced at him and saw that he seemed to have paled several shades. He looked completely aghast at the idea and she felt a moment's misgiving, but she quickly squelched it.

"Just stay here with Rio. When I say the word, he can pull the cow far enough for her to find purchase."

"No! Absolutely not." He came and stood in front of her, blocking her access to the water. "It's just a damn heifer. Not worth your life."

"Yeah, but it's *my* damn heifer. And besides, nothing's going to happen to me."

"If *she* can fall through the ice, *you* can fall through the ice."

"She weighs a few pounds more than I do," Annie pointed out dryly. "The ice didn't hold her but that doesn't mean it won't hold me. Anyway, I have to try. Now get out of my way."

He didn't budge. "No. You'll have to get by me first."

He sounded like a character in one of those bad spaghetti westerns her dad used to watch. She sighed, hating the idea of pulling rank on him. But she'd rather do that than stand here helplessly while an animal suffered and died in front her.

"If you want a job tomorrow," she finally said quietly, "you'll get out of my way now."

He paused, his hands clenched tightly and his breathing huffing as hard as if he'd just run a marathon, then he stepped away, impotent fury in his gaze. "Fine. Don't blame me if you die out there."

She bit her lip, fighting a sudden, hysterical urge to laugh. "I won't, I swear. If I die, you'll be the last one I blame."

In an effort to distribute her weight, she dropped to her stomach on the ice, feeling the cold seep through her heavy layers of clothing. With the rope tightly in her hand, she slowly, carefully, commando-crawled the twenty feet toward where the cow had crashed into the water, praying all the way that the ice would hold.

She had to be crazy. Luke was right, it was just one cow. She had hundreds more.

But she had given up too many times before. After the first few years of her marriage, she had grown so tired of fighting that she had eventually just quietly surrendered. Her will, her self-respect, her spirit.

She wouldn't do it again.

With fresh determination, she inched the final few feet to the cow, her heart pounding thick and fast in her chest and her senses heightened by adrenaline.

Pitching and thrashing, the animal bawled in terror and rolled her eyes back in her head.

"Easy now," Annie crooned softly. "That's the way. Take it easy, sweetheart."

She studied the situation and the best way to reach her objective. She couldn't throw the rope from down here on her stomach but she hesitated to stand and put her weight all in one spot.

She decided she could risk being on her knees. It was awkward looping the lariat from down here but she tried to remember everything Colt and Joe had ever taught her about using a rope.

Her first throw missed the cow completely but she forced herself to patiently coil the rope again and start all over. This time her meticulous efforts were rewarded. This second attempt was textbook perfect, sailing square over the Hereford's horns, and she pulled the rope taut.

"Yes!" Luke yelled from the shore, his huff apparently forgotten, and Annie grinned at him over her shoulder. She wanted to jump up and perform a little victory dance but decided it probably wouldn't be the wisest thing in the world when she was literally on thin ice.

"Should I back him up now?" Luke called from Rio's side.

"Not yet. Wait until I'm out of the way."

She dropped to her stomach again and started to crawl back the way she had come, feeling inordinately proud of herself. She had done it. She had actually done it!

But when she was still only halfway to shore, that pride turned to alarm. She heard a huge crash behind her and whipped her head around just in time to see the cow lunge through the ice, using the extra leverage afforded her by the rope in her panic to be free of the water.

Annie tried to slide out of the way but she wasn't fast enough. She felt the ice shudder, heard an ominous crack, and the next thing she knew, she was in the water.

Cold.

Breath-stealing, mind-numbing cold.

The water wasn't deep here, probably only about six feet, but it was still over her head.

The layers of heavy clothing that had seemed so comforting earlier in the day now acted as an anchor, pulling her down, down, and for one panicked second she couldn't move, tangled amid her coat and sweater and shirt. Then, with a mighty heave, she fought her way back to the surface.

She came up gasping and choking, conscious only of

the cold freezing her muscles and snatching away any air she could force into her lungs.

She was going to die here, in this frigid water. She was going to lose everything important to her—C.J. and Leah, the ranch, Joe—because of one stupid cow.

Not if she could help it. She gripped the edge of the ice so she wouldn't go down again and hung on with all her might.

"Annie?" Luke called. "Can you hear me?"

She tried to answer him but couldn't draw enough air in to her tortured lungs to make her vocal cords work so she just nodded her head, hoping he could see her.

"I've got the rope here. I took it off the cow and now I'm gonna try to toss it to you. Can you catch it?"

She nodded again, then waited while he looped it over his head and tossed it. This time, he did what he hadn't been able to do in a dozen tries with the cow and managed to throw where he was aiming, just inches away from her.

She reached for it and tried to twist her hands around it but her fingers were numb, unwieldy, and she couldn't hang on.

Tears of frustration welled up in her eyes when the rope slipped out of her hands.

"Come on, Miz Annie." Luke called, sounding on the verge of tears himself. "Come on. You can do it."

She tried. She really tried. Through three more tosses of the lariat she would catch hold of the rope but couldn't keep her fingers around it enough for Luke to pull her out of the water.

She had probably been in the water only a few moments but it felt like hours. Days. By the fifth throw, her muscles had gone rigid, uncooperative, and she felt her vision dim around the edges.

Just when she was beginning to think it wouldn't be so terrible to just slide into the icy depths, a miracle burst through the trees.

He loved it up here in the winter.

This corner of Montana was beautiful throughout every season but Joe had always found a special peace and solitude up here in wintertime, when the mountain slept and the only sounds came from the wind mourning through the pines and the high cry of a hawk soaring the air currents along the high ridgeline.

Quixote picked his way carefully through the snow, following the trail forged by a snowmobile—maybe even the very one he'd seen from the ranch. Joe could also see that two horses had come this way sometime after the snowmobiler, judging by the way the tread pattern had been disturbed by horse hooves.

Not that he was a tracking expert. That was just a stereotype. Folks tended to think just because he had Native American blood he automatically possessed some magical, mystical gift that allowed him to read trail sign. The funny thing was, everything he knew about nature and his place in it he'd picked up from Bill McKendrick, Colt's father.

He laughed to himself at the irony just as he breached the top of the mountain. Through the trees, he could see the snow-covered Butterfly Lake, nestled in a bowl-shaped cirque on the mountain exactly halfway between the Double C and the Broken Spur.

Most of his best memories were connected to this place somehow. He and Colt and Annie had considered it their own private domain, although technically it was part of the surrounding national forest. The three of them spent hours up here, fishing, cooking foil-wrapped hobo dinners over a fire, and camping—minus Annie, usually, since her dad wouldn't allow it.

He remembered she had defied her father and come with them only once, the summer she was eleven. She had snuck away from the Double C and spent the whole evening jittery and anxious, watching the trail for any sign of her father. Probably hadn't enjoyed a minute of it.

He asked her the next day how hard her whipping had been. To his astonishment, she shook her head and said she hadn't gotten a whipping. Her father had only told her he was disappointed in her.

At the time, Joe couldn't believe any father could be so lenient. He thought she must be the luckiest kid in the world. If it had been Albert Redhawk doling out the punishments, she wouldn't have been able to sit down for at least a couple of weeks.

But now he could see that Samuel Calhoun's brand of punishment left just as many scars. He had *always* been disappointed in Annie and she had spent her whole life trying to change that.

Qui started down the other side of the steep trail. Joe was careful to keep the horse to the inside of the trail, as far as he could get from the steep drop-off. He knew that the slightest misstep could send both horse and rider hurtling over the edge.

He was so busy watching the snowy trail that he didn't see the drama unfolding below him until he was almost halfway down. Through a break in the trees, he scanned the little valley and saw a heifer floundering to break free of the ice.

Annie and Luke were on the shore of the lake, and from here they appeared to be arguing about something. He saw her toss her red head—and had just a moment to wonder where her blasted hat was—then he saw her grab something from Luke. He sat forward in the saddle trying to get a better look just as Annie pushed her way past the ranch hand and headed toward the ice.

His heart caught in his throat. She couldn't be. Surely she wouldn't be so foolhardy.

But she was.

He drew in a ragged breath as he watched her drop to her stomach and inch carefully out on the frozen lake, a rope in her outstretched hand.

He wanted to yell, to shout, to throw something at her to make her stop but he knew she wouldn't hear him from this distance, so he did the only thing he could. He spurred Quixote the rest of the way down the trail, heedless now of the dangerous conditions.

Because of the trees towering on either side, he couldn't tell what was happening below until he reached the bottom of the trail. The first thing he saw was the stray cow, now standing casually near the trees nudging her calf as if nothing had happened.

Then he saw Annie in the water.

Panic washed over him colder than any glacial lake and he jumped from his horse and raced toward the ice.

Luke caught sight of him when he was still a few yards away. The kid looked like he was going to start blubbering any second now.

"I tried to stop her, Joe!" he cried. "I swear I did. She wouldn't listen to me! If she had listened to me, everything would have been fine."

"Annie!" he shouted. "Hang on, sweetheart."

"I tried to get her to grab the rope but her hands kept slipping off."

"So why the hell didn't you go in after her?" he growled, throwing off his hat and coat.

"I...I was just getting ready to do that," Luke mumbled, but Joe barely heard him, consumed only with Annie and the way her efforts to break free seemed to grow more feeble by the second.

He grabbed the rope from Luke, grateful somebody had at least had the foresight to tie one end to Annie's horse. He tied the other end around his waist then dropped to his stomach and slithered out to her

"It's c-c-cold," she whimpered when he neared her.

"I know, sweetheart. Hang on. We'll get you out of there."

He knew the tricky part would be near the jagged edge where she had fallen through the ice. It would be weak and unstable and probably wouldn't support his weight.

Ordinarily, he would have tried to extend a branch for her to grab hold of, but if she couldn't hang on to the rope, she wouldn't be able to hang on to a branch.

But he could hang onto her and that's what he decided to try. "Can you give me one of your hands?"

She nodded and held a slim, painfully white hand out of the water. He gripped her wrist tightly. His touch probably hurt like hell but it sure beat the alternative. Dying.

"Good girl. I'm going to give you a tug so you can get back on the ice, okay?"

She didn't even nod this time, just looked at him with complete trust in her eyes. Straining every muscle, he pulled as hard as he could against her waterlogged weight, afraid he was going to yank her shoulder out but knowing he didn't have a choice.

She slid from the water suddenly and flopped onto the ice, then she was in his arms.

He thought they were home free from there. They

GET FREE BOOKS
and a
FREE GIFT WHEN YOU PLAY THE...

LAS VEGAS GAME

Just scratch off the gold box with a coin. Then check below to see the gifts you get!

YES!

I have scratched off the gold Box. Please send me my **2 FREE BOOKS** and **gift for which I qualify.** I understand that I am under no obligation to purchase any books as explained on the back of this card.

▼ DETACH AND MAIL CARD TODAY! ▼

345 SDL C6RA

245 SDL C6Q5
(S-IM-OS-02/01)

NAME	(PLEASE PRINT CLEARLY)

ADDRESS

APT.# CITY

STATE/PROV. ZIP/POSTAL CODE

7	7	7	Worth TWO FREE BOOKS plus a BONUS Mystery Gift!
🍒	🍒	🍒	Worth TWO FREE BOOKS!
🔔	🔔	♣	TRY AGAIN!

Offer limited to one per household and not valid to current Silhouette Intimate Moments® subscribers. All orders subject to approval.

should have been. But the combined weight of both of them was more than the weakened ice could hold. Before he could catch his breath or even give her a reassuring squeeze, they were in the icy water.

How had she stood it, even for the few minutes she'd been in the frigid lake? He gasped, fighting to take a breath, and kept his arms around her tightly.

Fortunately, for once Luke was smart enough to do exactly what needed to be done. He slowly backed up Rio. Joe felt a tug on his waist as the rope went taut, then the horse dragged them free of the water, back onto the ice, then to the shore.

He lay there in the snow for a moment, soaked and freezing, with Annie still tight in his arms.

He wanted to shake her until her teeth rattled out of her head and then he wanted to kiss her and never, never stop.

The force of the impulse stunned him. So much for working to control his emotions. He had about as much control of them as he did those ice floes out there.

"Th…thanks," she gasped out, then coughed up a mouthful of lake water and he knew he couldn't afford to stay here even long enough for his heart to start again.

The water had been bitter cold but being out of it was worse. An icy wind cut through their wet clothes, stabbing them with a thousand blades. Already Annie's lips had gone beyond blue. They looked completely bloodless and she was shaking uncontrollably.

As much as he wanted to tear a strip or two out of her hide for doing something so crazy, it would have to wait until he could get her out of those wet clothes and into something warm.

Riding the two miles back to the Double C in her

condition would finish the job the icy water had started, he knew. It would be much closer to take her to the old Broken Spur line shack, halfway up the cirque.

When he was foreman for Colt, he always kept it well-stocked with blankets, food and a first aid kit in case of emergencies. He hoped like hell Colt had continued the tradition.

Knowing he didn't have much time, that she was already hypothermic and he was well on the way, he whistled for Quixote then scooped Annie out of the snow.

"Up you go now." He handed her into the saddle. "We'll get you warmed up in two shakes."

"Is she gonna be okay?"

Joe glanced over to find Luke Mitchell still looking white and scared.

"I think she will be as soon as she gets warmed up. I'm going to take her up to the line shack so I can get her out of the wind. Take her horse and ride on back to the house and let them know what's happened. Then send Manny or Luis out here on one of the sleds with some dry clothes."

Luke nodded and mounted up, then turned back to Annie. "I'm real sorry this happened, Miz Redhawk."

"It's not your fault," she answered through chattering teeth. "You tried to talk me out of going out."

But he still looked guilty, almost ashamed. "I didn't want something like this to happen. I could've roped her if you'd given me one more chance."

Joe didn't give her time to respond, just spurred Qui up the mountainside toward the line shack.

"How's my heifer?" she asked fretfully.

Leave it to Annie to worry more about a cow than she did about herself. If not for the stupid animal, she wouldn't have been in this mess in the first place. "She'll be fine. On her way to a warm bed back at the barn, I imagine."

She turned her head to look behind them and offered a weak smile at the sight of the cow and her calf hurrying to keep up with Luke.

"Good," she said softly. "That's good." And then she resumed her silent shaking.

Chapter 10

She never knew it was possible to be so cold.

Living through thirty-two Montana winters had given Annie plenty of experience in bitter temperatures—early mornings when she had to chop through six inches of ice in the water troughs so the stock could drink, when her gloves would stick to any surface they touched, when the air was so clear and so frigid that every sound seemed to carry for miles.

But she had never been as bone-deep cold as she was right now. Every breath was torture, as if her lungs were caught in a vice lined with razor blades that sliced tighter with each inhalation.

Her wet hair had frozen solid now they were out of the water and she could hear it crackle when she turned her head, which she didn't do much since even the slightest movement sent stinging pain cutting through every nerve ending.

She clung to the saddle with fingers that had long ago

lost sensation, afraid that if she let go she would fall to the ground and shatter into a million tiny, jagged shards of ice.

Just when she wasn't sure she could make it another step, the small line shack appeared through the trees. Its simple log walls matched the weathered gray of the tree trunks all around but was more glorious to her than any grand cathedral.

"Here we are," Joe said behind her.

She was mortally terrified she wouldn't have the strength to dismount by herself but he took the dilemma out of her hands by lifting her down, just as if she weighed nothing and wasn't encumbered by another thirty pounds of ice-crusted clothing.

The door to the line shack wasn't locked and the interior was even more humble than the outside. The air smelled dank with disuse and the one-room shack had few furnishings—just an iron bedstead, an old plank table with a couple of rickety chairs and a few crates nailed to the wall for storage.

She thought it looked wonderful, especially after Joe went to one of the crates and pulled out a pile of blankets.

"Remind me to buy Colt a beer," he said. "Dry firewood already laid out in the woodstove, warm blankets to bundle up in, even a kerosene lantern. All the comforts of home."

He handed her two fatigue green army surplus blankets and a brightly colored wool one with a slit in the middle to be worn like a poncho. A ruana, Manny and Ruben called them. "Here, take off those wet clothes and wrap up in these while I try to start a fire."

She tried to do as he said. She really did. But in the short time it took him to light the lantern and coax a merry little blaze to life in the potbellied stove, she had only been able to take off her coat and pull her sweater over her head.

The buttons on her soaking wet cotton work shirt and on her blue jeans completely defeated her stiff, unwieldy fingers.

He added a medium-sized log to the stove, then turned back to her, his hands on the buttons of his own wet shirt. When he saw she hadn't made much progress, he frowned.

"Why are you just standing there? You need to get out of your clothes. All of them."

"I can't," she murmured, and the words tasted as bitter as willow bark.

"Why not?"

She bit her tongue, loathe to tell him the truth. She was so pitiful. Any lingering sense of accomplishment she had felt in throwing the rope around that heifer out on the ice completely disappeared.

All she had succeeded in proving was once again how totally inept she was. And she had nearly killed them both in the bargain.

Now she couldn't even get undressed without help.

Before she could swallow her pride enough to ask for help, Joe figured out her dilemma on his own, his eyes widening as realization dawned. "You stubborn woman," he muttered. "You should have said something."

He came to stand in front of her, so close she could feel heat emanating from him even through his own wet clothes. As gently and dispassionately as if she were a child—as if he hadn't explored her mouth with his just the week before—he worked the buttons of her shirt free.

Maybe it was because she had just escaped death but everything suddenly seemed much more intense to her—the black of his eyes, the glide of his skin against hers, the smell of him, of leather and sage and Joe.

She couldn't seem to look away from the movements of his hands, at the contrast between his dark fingers and the lighter fabric of her shirt. They moved so elegantly, so beautifully, and by the time he worked free the button-fly of her jeans, she felt much, much warmer.

He reached to pull her jeans off her hips and a flush crawled over her cheeks, of embarrassment and of awareness.

She stepped away quickly and cleared sudden hoarseness from her throat. "I think I can manage from here. Thanks."

"Are you sure?"

She nodded and turned her back to him, feeling extremely foolish as she carefully eased off the wet shirt and her long underwear top. Hot needles of sensation began to return to her fingers as she pulled the ruana over her head then shimmied out of her soaked jeans and wrapped another blanket around her hips.

She was completely covered, but she still felt exposed, vulnerable, alone here with him in this small cabin.

The sides of the poncholike ruana would have gaped open but she kept them tightly tucked under her arms as she carried her wet clothing toward the glorious warmth beginning to emanate from the woodstove.

Taking great care to keep her face averted from the corner where he was shrugging out of his own wet clothes, she hung her jeans and shirt over one of the chairs then set her socks and boots on the stone hearth to dry.

Joe had spread another blanket from the dwindling supply on the ground to take the chill from the bare wood floor and Annie sank down gratefully and began to dry her hair with a corner of the ruana.

"How are you doing?"

She glanced up. Joe was dressed the same way she was, with one blanket around his hips and another wrapped around his shoulders.

The sight only seemed to reinforce the intimacy of their situation. They were completely alone here in this little cabin—sheltered from the winter winds, dressed in only a few layers of cloth and with the room bathed in just a dim circle of light from the kerosene lantern on the table.

She swallowed. "Better. Still cold but at least I know I still have fingers and toes."

"Are you hungry? I could heat some soup. That might help warm you up from the inside out."

She shook her head. "I'm afraid my stomach is still too twitchy to hold anything down. Maybe in a little while."

He hung his clothes on the other chair. Then, because there was nowhere else to sit, he folded his long length beside her on the blanket, bringing his heat to add to the fire's glow.

They sat next to each other for a few moments, not touching. Even without physical contact between them, she had never been more painfully aware of him. No matter how hard she tried to wrench her mind away from it, she was lost in the memory of their kiss the week before, of the heat and magic of his mouth dancing on hers.

She pulled the ruana more closely around her. "How long do you think it will be before help gets here?"

"An hour, hour and a half, maybe. With the sun down, whoever comes up will have to move slowly."

"The kids are probably worried sick."

"Patch will take care of them. He was just heading over to the house when I saddled Qui for the ride up."

"I hate not being there when they get home from school."

Anger suddenly kindled in his dark eyes. "Maybe you should have thought about that before you decided to risk your stubborn little neck taking a dip in a frozen lake. A few more moments out there and you might have missed being there after school permanently."

She stiffened, disliking the guilt sparked by his words. She *had* been reckless and stupid, but she didn't need him rubbing it in. "I did think about them."

"Not long, I imagine. If you had given your children more than two seconds of thought, I doubt you ever would have gone out on that ice."

"I thought it would hold."

"You thought wrong, didn't you?"

She glared at him. "What would you have me do? Let that heifer drown? You would have done exactly the same thing. I know darn well you would have."

He was silent for a moment while the fire crackled and hummed, then finally he shrugged. "Maybe. That doesn't mean you made the right choice. Dammit, Annie, you should have known better."

Despite his scolding tone, some of the triumph that had soared through her out on the ice returned.

Suddenly she wanted desperately to share that thrill of accomplishment. "I had her, Joe. You should have seen it, the way that rope sailed right around her neck, just like I was calf-roping in the rodeo."

"Don't sound so proud of yourself," he muttered darkly. "You nearly got yourself killed."

"I *was* proud of myself. For once, I felt like I finally did something right. Until the ice cracked, anyway."

He sent her a puzzled sidelong glance. "You do plenty of things right on the Double C."

"Not enough," she muttered.

He frowned. "What do you mean by that?"

"Nothing. Never mind."

"Tell me."

"I hate always feeling so lost. So afraid." The words rushed out of her before she could call them back.

He stared at her. "What are you talking about?"

She closed her eyes, mortified at herself. Whatever had possessed her to say such a thing?

If they had been under any other circumstances, she wouldn't have dreamed of sharing her most secret fears. But here, alone in this cabin bathed only by low lantern light, the protective layer she always tried to keep around herself cracked apart just as the ice had done earlier.

"Nothing," she said again, wanting to pull the wool ruana over her head and hide away from him. "Forget I said anything."

"Annie, I won't forget it. Tell me what you meant by that. What are you afraid of?"

She peered through her lashes and saw astonishment and consternation in his dark eyes and she knew with conviction that he wouldn't let the matter drop until she answered him.

She debated lying to him but there were too many lies, too many secrets, between them already.

"Everything," she finally said quietly, starkly. "I'm afraid of everything. That I'm fooling myself thinking

I can run the Double C. That everyone will discover how completely, totally inept I am at everything. And that someday Leah and C.J. will hate me for the choices I've made.''

Joe stared at her, stunned by the raw self-doubt in her voice. What had happened to his fearless little Annie who used to charge into every situation with fists raised and that stubborn, ''watch-out'' tilt to her chin?

Pain gnawed at his stomach. He knew exactly what had happened to her. His brother. Charlie had told her she was worthless so often that she had finally begun to believe him. Even her father hadn't been able to accomplish that.

Familiar, impotent fury at his brother warred with the need to comfort her, to take her pain away. ''Annie—''

She shook her head and he saw tears spilling onto her lashes before she blinked them back. ''Don't say a word. Not one word. I shouldn't have opened my big mouth. Just forget I said anything.''

How could he forget? She had just exposed her soul to him, the first time she had been so brutally honest with him since before she married Charlie. He couldn't just pretend nothing had happened.

He reached out and folded one of her still-icy hands into his. He would have kissed it if he wasn't afraid the gesture would look totally ridiculous—he would never be a hand-kissing kind of guy—so he gave it a squeeze instead. ''You amaze me, Annie,'' he murmured.

The confused wariness in her eyes broke his heart into tiny little pieces and made him realize he had slipped up badly. He had been so busy trying to help her put her ranch back together that he hadn't paid much attention to ensuring she did the same to herself.

He, of all people, should have been aware of the tumult she must have been going through.

That word she'd used—*lost*. That was exactly how he had felt after he got out of the state pen in Deer Lodge, as if he were wandering alone in a dark and frightening place full of unfamiliar landmarks and bizarre emotions.

He had always thought that no one else could begin to understand it, that bitter shame. The irrational fear that everywhere he went, people could smell the bleak stench of prison on him and would know where he had come from, what he had been.

He had floundered for months, years even. Hell, he still felt lingering traces of that inadequacy, that disgrace. Why else was he so dead-set on taking this job in Wyoming?

Both of them had chosen their prisons, he when he pleaded guilty to killing his father and Annie when she married Charlie. But they had each served their sentences, had regained their freedom, and now they needed to make the most of what they had left.

Neither of them could do that when their minds were still locked in those dark, miserable cells.

He blew out a breath, wishing he was better with words and could know the right ones to somehow make everything better.

"If anyone can handle running the Double C, it's you, Annie," he finally said. "You just need to have a little faith in yourself."

"Easier said than done," she mumbled.

"Take it from your foreman, you're a damn fine rancher. You work harder than any of your hands, so hard it worries me sometimes—I'm afraid you're going to wear yourself right out."

She shook her head in denial but he could see color had climbed her face at his words.

He squeezed her hands again. "I mean it, Annie. You have nothing to feel inadequate about. You have great instincts when it comes to your stock, you care about every animal and person in your operation—which is more than I can say about most ranchers—and in the eighteen months I've been here, I've agreed with every single decision you've made about the Double C."

He gave a rueful smile. "Except for today, when you headed out onto that ice."

She made a face, then smiled back at him and for a moment she looked exactly like the beautiful, vibrant girl he had kissed on the shores of Butterfly Lake so many years before.

He wanted to kiss her again. The need punched him in the chest, in the gut. He wanted to tug her toward him and consume that mouth, to taste her sweetness and feel her come to life in his arms.

He could do none of those things. Kissing her the morning after Dolly's poisoning had been a disastrous mistake, a mistake he had just spent one week regretting—at least when he wasn't reliving every moment of it in bittersweet detail.

He needed to let go of her fingers. Now.

He knew it perfectly well. But knowing it and doing it were two vastly different things. He couldn't seem to make his muscles cooperate, couldn't seem to do anything but sit there and stare at her while her fingers fluttered in his.

It didn't help his self-control any knowing both of them were just a couple of layers away from being bare, that there was tantalizing skin somewhere underneath that brightly colored wool.

He cleared his throat, fully intending to retreat. Before he could move, though, his gaze met hers and the awareness blooming there in those soft green depths was more than he could withstand.

He thought of how close she had come to death out there on the ice, how this brave, foolish woman would have perished for a cow, and he knew he couldn't fight it anymore.

Just a quick kiss, he promised himself. That's all he wanted. Just enough to get it out of his system so he could once more regain his balance and remember all the reasons they shouldn't be doing this.

But the instant his lips met hers, everything changed.

Her mouth was warm and willing beneath his and she made a soft, erotic little sound of welcome. Red-hot desire scorched through him at the sound, at the sweet taste of her, and he groaned and deepened the kiss.

Their mouths tangled in an explosion of need, hers soft and yielding, his hard and demanding.

They knelt chest to chest, hip to hip, and he was vaguely aware of the blanket slipping from his shoulders when her trembling fingers wandered up to splay against his bare chest. He had to close his eyes as sensation after sensation poured over him.

She was alive—they were both alive—and his body cried out with the need to celebrate that in the most elemental of ways.

Between the loose folds of the poncho he easily found the soft curve of her breast. She inhaled sharply when his fingers caressed her bare skin.

She went rigid in his arms and for one brief, terrible moment he thought she was going to pull away from him. But then her body seemed to sigh in surrender, to melt against him.

With their mouths entwined, with the fire popping and hissing beside them, he pushed her back to the blanket on the floor. She went willingly, sliding her arms around him to hold him close. His chest rubbed against the wool covering her and even that friction was too much. He wanted—needed—to feel skin on skin.

She must have had the same instinct. Before he could do anything to pursue the need, she broke the connection of their mouths to whip the wool over her head.

His breathing harsh, he gazed at her in the soft glow of the lantern. She was exquisite, with ivory skin and fine, delicate bones. His hands felt entirely too rough, too big, to touch such fragile skin. But how could he stop when she arched against him like that, when she gasped his name as his fingers closed around her?

One corner of his mind, the sensible part, warned that this was madness, that he was torturing himself with something he would only regret later. The rest of him told the killjoy to shut the hell up.

His body surged with need as he kissed her again, as his hands caressed her skin. He wanted to taste that skin, those taut, hard peaks. Before he could, though, the roar of a snowmobile coming up the hillside pierced the thin walls of the shack.

Both of them froze for one brief, charged second. Then Joe, shocked back into his senses, drew back. He grabbed the ruana from the floor and yanked it back over her head, forcing himself not to look at her face, at the condemnation he was afraid he would find there.

What the hell had he just done? It was bad enough he'd kissed her at all, but in another few moments he would have taken things much, much further. After a few more of those heated caresses he wouldn't have been able to stop himself from taking her right there on the floor.

"Annie, I..." He raked a hand through his hair, not sure what he wanted to say. "I'm sorry" would have been a blatant lie. He should have been sorry and he knew he would have plenty of regrets later. But now all he could feel was the pulse of desire still pounding through him.

"You don't have to say anything," she said, her voice low. "I understand. We were both overwrought from what happened out there on the ice. Both just glad to be alive. It doesn't mean anything."

Tell that to his heart, he thought as he went to open the door for their rescuers.

Chapter 11

"Here. This is all of it. Are you happy now?"

With an inward sigh, Annie took the stack of papers from her daughter's outstretched hand and refrained from warning her to watch her snippy tone of voice. "Thank you," she murmured instead.

Leah's posture screamed impatience, from the frustrated set of her jaw to the way she shifted from foot to foot in those expensive high-tops she insisted on buying with her baby-sitting money, shoes that were totally impractical for a snowy Montana winter.

"This will just take a moment," Annie said.

"You're going to make me late for the bus."

If Leah had given her the homework forty-five minutes earlier, when Annie had first asked to see it, being late for the school bus wouldn't even be an issue.

Again she swallowed the words, knowing they would only spark full-scale fireworks. "You still have at least ten minutes before the bus comes. It shouldn't take me that long to review your work. And if you miss the bus, I promise I'll drive you into town.''

''What about me?'' C.J. asked around a mouthful of oatmeal topped with enough strawberry jam to draw every grizzly in Montana.

''You have no excuse, young man. I already looked at your homework last night, so if you miss the bus you're walking.'' She smiled at him to let him know she was teasing.

He grinned back. ''Maybe I'll ride one of the horses to school like you did in the old days.''

Annie laughed. ''I'm not *that* old. We had school buses in my day.''

Before C.J. could answer, Leah gave a loud, impatient sigh. Annie raised an eyebrow at her daughter's lack of subtlety but returned to the stack of homework papers.

''This is excellent!'' she said after a few moments. ''Leah, I can't believe this! You haven't missed a single question.''

''I was lucky.''

''No you weren't. You worked hard. I'm so proud of you! It took me months to figure out integers and you've conquered it in just a few days. Way to go! I knew you could do it.''

A flush sneaked over the high cheekbones Leah inherited from her father. ''It's just a stupid math assignment,'' she mumbled, thrusting the homework back into a folder then shoving it all into the big, slouchy bag she carried. ''Get over it.''

Though her words were irritated, Annie knew her daughter well enough to tell she was pleased by the praise.

''I won't get over it. I hope this teaches you that you

can handle every one of your classes if you just put a little work into it. I'm proud of you," she said again.

"Does that mean I can ride Stardust again?"

For a moment, Annie almost gave in to the naked pleading in her voice. Leah loved that horse more than she loved anything and Annie knew the last month of being without her had been torture.

On the other hand, she wasn't sure if a few isolated weeks of turning in homework on time—due to much hounding from her mother—really qualified as bringing up her grades.

She hated this part of parenting. She hated being the disciplinarian, the enforcer, especially when her instincts cried out to do everything she could for her children to make up for a past filled with such stress.

She wanted to be the best-friend kind of mom who made pancakes with blueberry syrup every morning, the kind of mom who could spend all her time doing everything within her power to make her children happy. She wanted to be able to give them anything they could ever want.

But she knew that would accomplish nothing. If anything, Leah and C.J. needed loving structure and rules more than ever now. They needed to know what was expected of them and what wouldn't be tolerated.

In the end, she waffled. "We'll talk about it. Let's see how you do on your social studies quiz today and then we can discuss it tonight."

With a quick, happy smile that reminded Annie painfully of the sweet girl her daughter had been just a short time ago, Leah picked up her bag and hurried out the door.

"Hey, wait up!" C.J. pushed away his oatmeal bowl, threw on his coat and grabbed his backpack.

"'Bye, Mom," he shouted over his shoulder on his way out the door, leaving behind sudden, disconcerting silence.

Annie moved to the kitchen window and watched them walk toward the mailbox where the bus would pick them up.

She loved them so fiercely, sometimes she couldn't breathe around it.

She worried constantly about whether she was making the right choices in their upbringing. It would have helped so much to have someone else to share both the burden and the joy.

Not that her divorce changed anything in that department—she had always been on her own when it came to parenting. Charlie took no more notice of either one of them than he would a couple of insects crawling on the sidewalk.

She sometimes wondered what she would have done if he had. She knew she wouldn't have stayed in the marriage if he had threatened to hurt them in any way.

She wouldn't have hesitated, would have just gathered them up and escaped even if it meant handing over the Double C to him. Her children were far more important than the ranch.

But she had fooled herself into thinking the way Charlie treated her was separate from the children, that it had no impact on them.

It was a stupid and shortsighted conclusion, she could see that now. Of *course* they had been affected. How could they not be?

He had never hit her in front of them but they had to have seen the bruises. She just hoped she had been able to come to her senses in time before it could scar them forever.

C.J. reached down now behind his sister's back to scoop up a handful of snow. A smile quirked the edges of her mouth as she watched him form a snowball then take aim. Uh-oh. He was asking for trouble.

The missile hit Leah square in the middle of her back. From here, Annie could see her mouth open in a shriek, then she whipped around to glare at her little brother. C.J. giggled, even when Leah scooped up a snowball of her own and headed toward him.

Annie smiled softly. She sometimes had a hard time believing a union so twisted and ugly could have produced something as wonderful as C.J. It was a miracle, really.

She had been so afraid when she found she was pregnant that she would never be able to love this child who had been conceived through violence and force.

Oh, how she was wrong. From the moment she felt him move inside her, she had loved him. She had ceased to care how he had come to be.

He was so funny and sweet, with more compassion in his little heart than anyone else she had ever known. If anything, he was *too* compassionate. He felt things more keenly than others and she worried sometimes that he was too vulnerable to the inevitable cruelties of life.

All mother birds worried about their baby chicks falling out of the nest and tumbling to the ground. She just had to do her best to make sure he had the skills he would need to fly.

And he was going to have to fly now if he wanted to get away from his sister.

Snowball in hand, she came after him, laughing and more carefree than Annie had seen her in a long time. C.J. dodged around the big spruce tree out front but Leah was faster and sneakier. She went around the other direction for a frontal attack and launched the snowball at him. It hit him square in the face and Leah bent over with laughter.

C.J. just grinned at his sister, snow dripping from his face, as the bus pulled up to the mailbox with a screech of brakes Annie could hear even from inside.

Leah's long dark hair swung out behind her as she climbed onto the bus, her brother right behind her. She wasn't wearing a hat again, Annie observed with a sigh. It was a constant battle between them, just like everything else had turned into these days.

Her daughter had grown up in the last year. She was becoming a beautiful, willowy young woman with her father's dark eyes and high cheekbones. Annie was amazed Leah and Joe couldn't see what was so glaringly obvious to her, but she thanked God for it every day.

Sometimes the weight of her secret felt like a thousand boulders she carried around with her every single waking moment. But it was a weight she must continue to carry alone. If either of them found out, she knew it would be devastating for everyone involved.

Neither one of them would forgive her for years of deception. Any more than she could forgive herself.

Even knowing she had had no choice—either in keeping the news of her pregnancy from Joe or in maintaining the pretense all these years that Charlie was Leah's father—she knew she would never be free of the remorse.

She sometimes felt as if the guilt would burn a raw, gaping hole in her stomach. She would rather endure it, though, would rather try to calm it with wagonloads of antacids, than have to face Joe and Leah with the truth.

The school bus pulled away, leaving only a wisp of

diesel exhaust in the cold morning air. She watched until even that dissipated, then turned away from the window.

She had too much to do to stand here all day worrying about things she couldn't fix.

She spent the morning doing as little housework as she could get away with so she could turn her attention to the omnipresent paperwork of the ranch.

Several hours later, she stood to stretch and realized it was almost lunchtime. Drat. She had planned to make a lunch for Patch.

The old cowboy was laid up in the bunkhouse since Maggie had finally given him an ultimatum—either he took it easy on his hip for a few days while things were slow at the ranch or she was personally going to drag him to the hospital in Billings for a hip replacement.

She hurriedly fixed a lunch, put it all on a tray, then headed outside. The day was colder than normal for early March but she thought she could smell the moist promise of spring.

March 10th. She thought of the date she had been writing on checks all morning. She had less than three weeks before Joe's departure. The bleak realization inevitably reminded her of the day two weeks before when she had fallen through the ice then caught fire in his arms.

Since then he had done his best to avoid her, always choosing any job that would take him away from the ranch. Today he had taken Luke and the Santiagos to a stock sale in Bozeman. But if they hadn't gone there, he probably would have found some other excuse to stay as far away from her as he could.

He hadn't said two words to her after they changed into the dry clothes Manny brought and started the long ride up the cirque then down the other side to the ranch. And he had barely said even that much in the weeks since.

She didn't have to be a genius to know he regretted kissing her, both times he had done it in the last month. He couldn't have made it more obvious.

It only took her a few moments to reach the bunkhouse but she hesitated on the step. One of her earliest lessons as a young girl growing up surrounded by a bunch of rough men was never to walk unannounced into the bunkhouse.

For all their bluster, cowboys could be as prissy as a bunch of schoolmarms when a woman invaded their territory.

At the same time, she knew if she rang the bell, Patch would try to get up to answer the door and she didn't want him to move more than he absolutely had to. Finally she compromised by knocking once then opening the door a crack.

"Patch? It's Annie," she called through the door. "Are you decent?"

The grizzled old cowboy's rusty-gate laugh met her question. "Not if I can help it, gal. Not if I can help it."

She smiled a little at the old joke and pushed the door completely open with her elbow. Inside the trailer was surprisingly homey considering it was decorated in bachelor chic.

Patch was lying on one of the mismatched couches, a soap opera on the big-screen TV and a western in his hand.

He scowled at the tray. "What the hell is that?"

She presented it for his inspection. "Lunch. Leftover chili and corn bread from dinner last night. A little early, I know, but I had a few extra minutes and figured I might be able to keep you from trying to get up to fix your own.''

His wrinkled old face twisted into a glare. ''I can take care of myself. Don't need no little girl doing it for me.''

''You know you're supposed to be resting. Maggie says if you don't take it easy for a few days, you're going to need a hip replacement by summer.''

He tossed his book down in disgust onto the old tack trunk that served as a coffee table in the bunkhouse. ''That gal needs to have that kid of hers so she'll keep her nose out of my business. I'm just fine and dandy. Too much to do around here for me to be sitting around on my rear end all day like some big baby. Don't blame me if the whole damn place falls apart.''

''I won't. I promise.'' She bit her lip to hide her grin and set the tray next to the discarded western. ''Since I went to all the trouble to fix it, you might as well eat it. I'll just put it here and then you can eat when you're hungry.''

''Suit yourself. You always did.''

This time she didn't bother to hide her smile as she bent to kiss his cheek above the handlebar of his mustache.

Her smile faded as she walked the short distance back to the house, back to her lousy paperwork.

Stubborn old mule.

If Patch didn't listen to Maggie and give his hip time to strengthen and heal, he wouldn't be able to ride a horse in another few months. What kind of fix would he be in if he couldn't do the only thing he loved? He would absolutely hate it. How could she convince him?

Worried and distracted, she opened the back door into

the mudroom and walked carefully, trying not to leave
tracks on the floor she had just cleaned.

Someone already had, she noticed with a frown. Big
ugly smears of mud were all over the floor leading into
the kitchen. She opened the door, so busy looking at
the mess on her floor that she didn't notice the figure
sitting at the kitchen table casually drinking a cup of
coffee until he spoke.

"Well, well, well. If it isn't my darling wife."

She stumbled and the empty tray in her hand clattered
to the floor. She would have fallen too but at the last
minute she reached a hand out to the counter to steady
herself.

"Ch…Charlie!"

"Did you miss me, sugar?"

She just stared at him. Her heart felt as if it would
pound through her rib cage and she could swear she
heard the roar of her blood in her ears. All the progress
she thought she had made toward rebuilding herself disappeared in an instant.

Still, it had to count for something that she was able
to swallow down the raw panic at least enough to speak
without even a quaver in her voice. "What are you
doing here?"

"Aren't you glad to see me?"

She wanted to scream and rage and throw that cup
of coffee all over him.

As she looked at his face—still chillingly handsome
but beginning to turn fleshy and soft—her skin felt
clammy, her stomach jittery.

She wouldn't let him do this to her again. Not anymore. She had broken free of him and she wasn't about
to give up all the progress she had made these nineteen
months.

Drawing on all the strength she could find, she crossed the kitchen to the telephone hanging by the refrigerator. With hands that only shook slightly, she lifted it off the receiver.

He chuckled. "Who you calling? Little Joey? Think he's going to come running to your rescue like he always did?"

"You're trespassing in my house. I'm calling Sheriff Douglas."

He slid the chair back with a screech that crawled down her spine like fingernails on a blackboard. "I wouldn't do that if I were you."

"You're not me."

And I'm not the stupid, scared little girl I was before. She quickly dialed the emergency number but before it could ring, Charlie reached out and pushed down the receiver.

"I said, I wouldn't do that if I were you."

Though his voice was completely without menace, Annie still shivered. She couldn't wrestle him for the phone—he was stronger than she was and almost twice as big. She couldn't even call for help—there was no one around to hear.

Why did he have to pick today of all days to show up on the ranch, when all the men were gone except Patch who was too far away to do anything, even if he hadn't been a seventy-year-old with a bad hip?

Maybe Charlie had planned it that way. Maybe he was the one she had felt watching her. Watching and waiting for a chance just like this, when he could catch her alone and unawares.

She felt herself begin to hyperventilate, felt the panic begin to take over, but forced herself to breathe deeply and evenly.

"What do you want, Charlie?" Her voice was harsh, guttural, not at all like her own.

"Geez, Annie. Relax. Can't a guy just come around to check on his family?"

"You don't have a family. Not anymore." *You never cared about the family you had while you were here.*

"How are the kids? The girl and little Charlie Junior?"

A chill started in her stomach and spread outward. "Fine. They're just fine."

"They ever ask about me?"

Where was this coming from? Charlie ignored both of the children when he lived here and she couldn't believe he would suddenly start caring about them after he left.

"No," she said abruptly.

He sat back down at the table and lifted the coffee cup to his mouth. "Well, that's too bad. I sure think about them. Especially my boy."

The chill seeped into her muscles, into her bones. "We had a deal, Charlie. You agreed to leave and not come back. You *agreed.*"

"Things change. People change."

"We had a deal." A deal she had paid for with her soul.

"I know. But see, I've got this hankering to get to know my boy. You wouldn't begrudge a father the right to know his kid, would you? I was thinking maybe I'd stick around for a while and get reacquainted with him."

You'll have to kill me first. She didn't say the words, maybe because deep down she was afraid Charlie would take her up on them.

"We had a deal. The warrant for your arrest is sitting

right on Sheriff Douglas's desk, just waiting to be executed. I'll give you one last chance to leave my house and then I'm calling him.''

"You don't have the guts. You never did."

She thought of her children. "Watch me, Charlie. Just watch me. I will not let you come back and destroy their lives. Not again."

His expression hardened. "You want to play hardball? Fine. We'll play hardball. Maybe I'll just go pick my kid up from school. He ought to be getting out in an hour or so. I'm sure he'd love the chance to catch up with the old man."

The chill changed to heat. Sick, greasy heat. She sank into a chair, one hand pressed to her stomach. "You... You'd be arrested before you even reached the school."

"Maybe. Maybe not. You willing to take that gamble?"

"What do you want? I know you don't give a damn about C.J. You never have."

He was quiet for a moment and then he gave that smile, the one that could charm just about everybody in the whole county. It only made her ill. "I was thinking it's time to renegotiate our little agreement."

Ah, here we go. The real reason he was here.

"Renegotiate?"

"I'm not sure I got my fair share for all the years I poured my sweat into this place."

Money. It always came down to money with Charlie. That was the reason he married her in the first place. She had just inherited a wealthy cattle ranch and he wanted it.

Not her. Never her. Just the ranch.

"I gave you everything the Double C could spare and

then some in the divorce settlement.'' Far more than he
deserved.

He leaned back in his chair. ''That was then. I hear
you've had a couple good years. My baby brother might
be a killer, but he does know cattle. Plus he's got you
spreading your legs for him like you always did to give
a little added incentive to perform.''

She drew in a ragged breath at his crudeness.

Charlie noticed her reaction, saw he'd pierced her
self-control and his mouth twisted into a satisfied smirk.
''Didn't mean nothing by that,'' he lied. ''Sorry. Whatever you and him do is your own business. But I figure
the ranch is still *my* business.''

''You signed documents saying otherwise. You gave
up any future claim to the Double C in the divorce.''

''Come on, Annie. Be reasonable for once. You can
spare a little more.''

''No. Absolutely not.''

He was quiet, ominously so, then his expression grew
even colder. ''You ever tell my little brother about his
bouncing baby girl?''

The blood seemed to seep from her face, the oxygen
from her lungs. ''What does that have to do with anything?''

''I'm sure he would just love to know the real reason
you entered into a life of marital bliss with me. I
wouldn't want to have to tell him how you came begging me to marry you so the kid he put in your belly
wouldn't have to grow up having to live with the shame
of everybody knowing her daddy was a killer.''

Here was his trump card, then. He could always pick
out her weaknesses. She knew Charlie wouldn't hesitate
to follow through with his threat. He would find sadistic
thrill in finally breaking the secrecy around Leah's pa-

ternity, would twist everything to make it sound sordid and ugly. And he wouldn't give a damn about the lives he shattered in the process.

She couldn't let him do it. No matter what, she couldn't let him destroy Leah and C.J. and Joe.

"How much?" she asked, in a voice just above a whisper.

He chuckled and raised the cup to her in a mocking salute. "I thought you'd see things my way, sugar. The way I figure it, a guy who's giving up his son ought to get something worthwhile for his trouble. How about, oh, maybe a hundred grand?"

She stared at him. "I don't have that kind of money just lying around! I can barely make payroll each month."

"Little brother must not be as good as I thought. Tell you what, we're running a special this week. How about you give me seventy-five and throw in the keys to that new pickup out there?"

"I don't have that much either!"

He shrugged. "What time does the girl get home from school? Should I tell her first or should I give the news to the proud daddy?"

She closed her eyes, defeated. This would never end, she thought in sudden despair. She would never, ever be free of him. "I'll do what I can," she whispered.

"I thought you would see things my way. Just to show you what a hell of a guy I still am, I'll give you a week to scrape it together. Does that sound fair?"

Numb, she just stared at him and he grinned, shoving his chair back from the table again. "I'll take that as a yes. See you next week, Annie, sugar. Pleasure doing business with you."

Chapter 12

She went through the motions of living the next six days in a fog, feeling as if a live grenade had fallen into her lap and was ready to explode any second.

So many things made a terrible kind of sense now—that eerie photograph, Dolly's poisoning, the downed fences. Charlie had to be behind all of it. He was obviously up to his old tricks, showing her he was still very much in control of her life and making sure she would never be able to find a moment's peace.

His ultimatum hung over her like a gray, ugly cloud and she felt paralyzed by indecision. How was she ever going to meet his demands? To come up with that much money?

A review of ranch accounts confirmed what she feared, that she could only raise half of what he was seeking without borrowing money or selling off some of the stock.

Neither option appealed to her much—she was already extended about as far as she dared go with the bank. And with beef prices so low right now and her cattle thinned by winter she would take a big hit hauling them off to market. It was time to buy, not time to sell.

Still, that seemed to be the best course of action, so she and Joe had just spent the afternoon trying to pick out twenty of her healthiest steers and tagging them for market.

He thought she was crazy. What else would he think? She couldn't tell him the truth. She couldn't possibly let him know why she needed to raise so much extra cash right now so she made up some story about not feeling the ranch had enough on hand for emergencies.

He didn't seem to be buying her excuse but he just shrugged and said she was the boss and she had the ultimate say.

Annie felt miserable lying to him and even more miserable that in only two more weeks the Double C and its cash reserves wouldn't be his problem anymore.

"Looks like we're due for a big one," Joe said now as they dismounted at the horse barn.

She frowned at him. "Why do you say that? We've seen better weather today than we have all winter."

All day a warm wind had been blowing out of the south, edging the mercury up into to the high forties for the first time since October and turning the Double C into a muddy, dripping mess.

Everywhere she went she heard the plop-plop of icicles melting, and the whole ranch—from the trucks to the cattle to her boots—was caked in cold, heavy muck.

"Spring's coming," she went on. "It's in the air."

"Not quite yet."

Joe pointed to a cluster of benign-looking clouds hovering around the Spanish Peaks. "In about an hour those clouds are going to let loose in a big way. Trust me.''

Trust me. The talk of storms drifted right out of her head as her mind caught on the words. She wished fiercely that she could trust him to forgive her if she ever told him the truth.

If she wasn't so afraid of his reaction, she would tell him herself and get it over with and then she wouldn't be going through this angst over Charlie's ultimatum.

She couldn't tell him, though. And she didn't deserve his forgiveness. She had deceived him for thirteen years, had stolen something precious and beautiful from him, and she deserved all the scorn and contempt he would feel if he ever uncovered her lies.

''Annie?''

She blinked and found him watching her with a perplexed look on his lean features. ''Did you say something?'' she asked.

''I said I'm afraid we're going to lose some of the calves up in the winter range unless we bring them closer to home. I can round up the boys and have them down here by the time the snow hits.''

''Whatever you think best,'' she mumbled distractedly.

He didn't answer her and after a few beats, she lifted her gaze to find him watching her out of those inscrutable dark eyes.

''Spill,'' he finally said. ''What's going on?''

Heat soaked her skin. She couldn't tell him. What would he do if he found out Charlie had come back?

There was no brotherly love lost between the two of them. She knew Joe had threatened his brother to within an inch of his life if he ever bothered her again. She didn't want to see him end up in jail over someone as worthless as Charlie.

"Nothing's going on," she lied.

"So what's with all the short answers and preoccupied looks you've been giving everybody for a week?"

"You're imagining things." She busied herself wrapping Rio's reins around the split rail fence next to Quixote.

"Is it Leah? Before he went to that sleepover at Nicky's house, C.J. told me she was in trouble again."

"Yeah. That must be it." She seized on the excuse, which wasn't exactly a lie. She *was* upset about Leah, she just had a hard time focusing on anything but Charlie and his threats.

"What's she done now?"

"She had her riding privileges back for not even a week when she skipped half a day of classes yesterday with some of her friends."

"Played a little hooky? Can't say I've never done that."

His mouth curved nostalgically for a moment. When his gaze met hers, he quickly straightened it out into a grave expression. "Which, of course, I deeply regret now."

"I don't understand her. She was supposed to be having a math test—she studied so hard for it—so why would she want to ruin all her progress by skipping class and not even taking the test?"

"Maybe she had her reasons. Did you ask her?"

"All we seem to do is yell. She's now grounded from riding that horse of hers for at least another month. I don't know any other way to get through to her."

He gazed out through the double doors of the horse barn and winced suddenly. "Looks like you'd better come up with something in a real hurry. The horse thing doesn't seem to be working.''

She followed the direction he was looking and her eyes widened in shock at the sight of Leah on her forbidden horse cantering toward them as if she didn't have a care in the world.

Annie reeled as if she'd been punched in the stomach. How could her daughter blatantly disobey her like this? Did Leah have so little respect for her that family rules meant nothing?

She could tell the instant Leah spotted them. Her smile faded, replaced by a pinched look of guilt and wariness.

Annie expected her to turn the horse around and flee but instead Leah stiffened her shoulders and reined in Stardust outside the barn then dismounted and led the horse into her stall just as if she had done nothing wrong.

"Easy," Joe murmured to Annie in a voice meant to calm her, but he could tell she barely heard him. She looked like she wanted to cry and he couldn't say he blamed her.

Leah was acting like a juvenile delinquent, flaunting rules and doing whatever she pleased. If she went on like this she was going to find herself in some serious trouble, if she wasn't already there.

He probably should leave. He didn't know if the instinct was self-preservation or just a natural desire to let Annie deal with her children in her own way.

But knowing mother and daughter shared the same temper, he thought he might be wise to stick around just in case things got too nasty and they needed a referee.

Annie took the offensive. "What do you think you're

doing, young lady?'' she said in an ominously quiet voice.

Defiance in every muscle of her body, Leah started removing the horse's tack. ''She needed exercise. She'll go soft if I don't work her.''

''You should have thought about that before you decided to skip class yesterday.'' Her shoulders slumped suddenly, and she looked completely miserable. ''Leah, I don't know what to do with you anymore. How can I get through to you?''

''How about not making up punishments that are totally stupid? Barring me from riding Stardust is not fair. She's my horse.''

''I'm just trying to make you realize that right now school is the most important thing in your life, whether you want it to be or not.''

''You don't care about school or whether I'm flunking out.'' Leah yanked the saddle off and threw it violently to the ground. ''You're just getting off on finally being able to push somebody else around for a change instead of you being the one getting pushed.''

Annie swayed as if her daughter had slapped her with more than just bitter words.

Okay, this was getting ugly. Time for the referee. ''That's enough,'' he said sharply.

Leah turned on him, her dark eyes glittering with tears. ''Stay out of this,'' she snapped. ''It's none of your business.''

''You think I'm going to stand here and let you be deliberately cruel to your mother? Think again. She didn't deserve that from you.''

''Yes she did. And you're as bad as she is.''

''Watch it, Leah,'' he snapped. ''You're not too big for me to turn over my knee.''

"What do you care?"

Tears dripped out of her eyes now and she sniffled loudly and wiped them with the sleeve of her coat. "You don't even care enough about me to tell me the truth. Either of you."

He frowned, baffled by the fury in her gaze aimed not only at her mother but at him. "The truth about what?"

"I know. You can stop with the lies now, both of you. I'm so sick of them I could scream. *I know everything.*"

Annie made a sudden distressed sound. He glanced toward her and saw that all the color had leached from her face, leaving her freckles standing out in stark contrast.

"You...you know what?" she whispered.

"I heard you and my...and Charlie fighting before he left for good. I heard everything. Were you ever going to tell me?"

Joe didn't know what the hell she was talking about but whatever it was, it sure was upsetting Annie. She looked so pale he was afraid she was about to pass out.

"I've been waiting ever since then for you to say something," Leah went on. "But I've finally figured out that you never planned to. Either one of you. You were both going to let me spend the rest of my life living a lie, weren't you?"

"Leah—" Annie began, but the girl turned away.

"I don't care. Do you hear me?"

She rushed to the door of the barn then turned back to face him, her face wet with tears. "I don't care that you're my real father. *I don't care!* I don't want you anymore than you wanted me."

With that bombshell, she ran out of the barn, leaving a stunned silence behind her.

Joe watched after her feeling as if the building had just toppled over on him.

Leah had to be mistaken. She *had* to be. No way in hell could he be her father.

But one look at Annie's pale face and trembling hands and he knew it was no mistake. She must have been conceived during their one and only time together, that afternoon of her father's funeral.

His hands shook badly as he raked both of them through his hair. "Is it true? She's mine?"

Silent tears coursed down Annie's cheeks and she was breathing as hard as if she had just wrestled a steer all by herself. "I didn't know what to do, Joe."

"You were pregnant and you didn't tell me?"

"How could I tell you? You left and then when you came back..." her voice trailed off.

"When I came back, I ended up in prison."

He drew in a ragged breath. He couldn't deal with this. In a matter of moments his whole life had been turned upside down and he just couldn't process it all right now.

And he especially couldn't face the woman he thought he had known, the woman he thought he had loved.

The woman who had lied to him for more than thirteen years.

"I have to go," he mumbled. He didn't trust himself to say anything else. Without looking at her again, he walked out of the barn.

After he left, Annie wanted to curl into one of the stalls and hide there forever. The grenade she had feared so much had finally exploded and now she had jagged

shards of shrapnel lodged in her heart, in her soul. With
every breath they drove in deeper.

She didn't know how long she stayed there, her arms
huddled around herself, her cheeks soaked with tears.

Eventually reality returned. She couldn't cower in
here for the rest of her life. She had spent enough time
hiding from the truth and now she had to face it head-
on.

She had to go after Leah. Her daughter would have
questions—how on earth had she kept them to herself
this long?—and Annie knew she owed her answers.

The first thing she noticed after she left the barn was
the cold. Just in the last few moments, the temperature
had dropped at least twenty degrees. An icy wind had
blown away the balmy promise of spring and now it bit
through her coat and shrieked under the eaves of the
barn. Just as Joe predicted, those ominous clouds had
moved closer—already a few icy crystals pelted her an-
grily.

The second thing she noticed was that both Rio and
Quixote were gone from where she and Joe had tied
them to the corral.

She frowned. Joe must have mounted up again after
he left the barn. She couldn't blame him. He probably
just needed to ride somewhere away from the ranch so
he could be alone to assimilate the news that he was
the father of a twelve-year-old girl.

She could understand why Qui was gone. That made
sense. But why would he have taken Rio, too?

She pushed the puzzle out of her mind. She had more
important things to worry about right now than a missing horse—like her daughter and the turmoil she had
somehow managed to keep hidden for so long, turmoil

that had obviously been at the root of her behavior problems.

Twenty minutes later, when she couldn't find Leah anywhere either inside the house or on the grounds, the missing horse took on a grim new significance.

Would Leah have taken Rio? And where would she have gone? Fear curled in her stomach. The storm was beginning in full force now. With that wind, the snow seemed to blow horizontally instead of vertically, until she could barely even see the house from here.

Annie didn't even want to think about all the things that might happen to a twelve-year-old girl out in the middle of a blizzard. Leah was a good horsewoman for a girl her age but she didn't have the coping skills to handle harsh weather like this.

She had to find her as soon as possible or Leah might not be able to make her way back.

Rushing to the horse barn, she started to saddle one of the other ranch horses, a big, brawny sorrel mare, when Joe came into the barn shaking snow off his slicker.

He stopped short when he saw her and she died a little inside at the fury and betrayal that leaped into his dark eyes. She forced herself to ignore it, though. She deserved every bit of his anger and then some.

"Where's Leah?" she asked urgently. "Is she with you?"

He shook his head. "I haven't seen her since she ran out of here earlier. Why?"

"Rio's gone. I think she took him. I think she's out there somewhere."

He growled a harsh oath. "That wind is a bitch. In another half hour visibility is going to be down to a few feet."

Fear clutched at her again but she tamped it down as she swung into the saddle. "Then let's hope I find her before then."

He held a hand on the bridle to hold the sorrel in place. "Don't do anything stupid. She probably just rode down to the mailbox or something and she'll be back in a few minutes."

"Maybe. But what if she's not? What if she's out there lost? I can't take that chance. It might be morning before it clears enough to look for her, otherwise."

"What the hell good would it do to go off looking for her if you only end up getting yourself lost too?"

"I know every inch of this ranch. I'm not going to get lost."

"Not in a blinding snowstorm you don't."

"It's my fault she's out there. I need to find her before the worst of the storm hits."

"She could be anywhere! We need to do this methodically, organize a search."

"In the time it would take to organize a search, who knows what could happen to her?"

"So you'd rather just wander out there aimlessly? Use your head, Annie!"

"I am using my head. Where does she always go when she's upset or in trouble? Up to the lake. I'm betting that's where she went this time."

He growled an oath. "God help her if she did. That trail is dangerous under the best of circumstances, which these definitely are not."

"I have to look for her, Joe."

He was silent for a moment then he let go of the horse's bridle. "Give me five minutes to round up the men and send them out looking closer to home and then I'll come with you."

* * *

Joe caught up with her just as she and the sorrel reached the High Lonesome trailhead.

"She might not even be up here," he called above the howl of the wind.

She pointed to the silent testimony embedded in the mud and snow in front of her—shod hoofprints leading straight up the trail. By the looks of it, the horse had been pushed through here hard fairly recently, since the snow hadn't had time to hide the trail away.

The screeching wind made speech next to impossible. Annie just hunkered down into her coat and concentrated on the difficult terrain and dwindling daylight, praying that Leah would be safe.

They saw no sign of her on the trail, nothing but those ghostly hoofprints beginning to disappear under the snow. By the time they rode down the lip of the bowl-shaped valley, her knuckles ached from holding tight to the reins and she couldn't see anything beyond the sorrel's ears.

They called Leah's name over and over but the wind snatched away their voices.

"Let's hope she had enough sense to hole up in the line shack," Joe shouted.

She nodded, but when they reached the shack a few moments later, they found it empty.

Disappointment and fear clutched at her. Where could she be? Breathing hard, Annie pushed past Joe to remount her horse, but he gripped her shoulders before she could.

"Annie, we're going to have to stop here, at least until the wind dies down a little," he shouted above the wind. "The horses are exhausted from fighting it and so are you."

"We can't stop! We have to find her. She's out there somewhere."'

He opened his mouth to argue with her but before he could, she caught a strange bleating sound on the wind. It sounded like it was coming from inside his coat.

He frowned, then reached into an inside pocket and pulled out one of the ranch cellular phones. It seemed so incongruous out here in the wilderness that for a moment she could only stare at him.

"Yeah?" he growled impatiently into the phone.

He was silent for a few moments then he answered but the wind snatched away his words. Through the whirling snow she could see him nod his head and then say something else before he ended the call and returned the phone to his pocket.

"That was Colt," he yelled to Annie. "She's safe."

Annie sagged against her horse. "Thank heaven! Where is she?"

"The reception was pretty choppy but I guess she's at the Broken Spur with him and Maggie and the boys. She never even made it to the lake, but ended up taking the fork in the trail to the Broken Spur before the worst of the storm hits. That's why we lost the hoofprints."

Relief poured over her, beautiful, warm cascades of it. "Is she hurt?"

"She's fine. Cold and wet and frightened, but fine."

Annie breathed another prayer of thanksgiving. "Let's go home, then," she shouted to him.

He shook his head. "I don't think so. It's too dangerous to try that trail again under these conditions. I think we need to hole up here through the worst of the storm and then head back to the ranch when it settles down a little."

The last thing in the world she wanted to do was

spend the night with Joe in the intimate confines of the line shack. Not with the emotional upheaval they both had been through that afternoon.

The thought of being alone with him terrified her, of being captive to a situation where they would have no choice but to talk to each other. He would demand answers from her. And how could she blame him? She had withheld the truth from him for more than thirteen years, he had a right to ask anything he wanted.

Even knowing he had the right to the truth, she wasn't sure how much she could—or would—be able to tell him about the choices she had made that summer.

But if she tried to go back down that slick trail in the middle of a howling blizzard, she risked serious injury—or worse.

As she walked inside the tiny confines of the line shack, she almost thought the risk would have been worth it.

Chapter 13

The line shack was cold, dark and unwelcoming.

Joe was grateful to whatever instinct had prompted him to replenish the supplies they had used two weeks before. He had come up himself earlier in the week to bring in more firewood and had returned the cleaned blankets to the crates nailed to the plank wall.

Now, while he found the kerosene lantern and followed the steps to coax it to life, he was supremely conscious of Annie watching him, wary and silent. In the low circle of light from the lantern, she looked pale and much, much too fragile to be riding out in the middle of a Montana blizzard.

He set the lantern on the table near her and she jumped suddenly at the thud of metal hitting wood.

He frowned. Why the hell was she acting afraid of him? Did she have so little faith in him, in his control over his emotions, that she actually thought he might hurt her?

He didn't think she could wound him any more but that did it. Of course she didn't have any faith in him. Otherwise she would have told him about Leah years ago instead of letting him find out like this.

His jaw flexed. He didn't know what was stronger in him right now, the amazement, the hurt, or the anger, this deep, aching fury that pulsed through him with every breath.

He thought they had cared about each other. They had been friends since they were kids—more than friends. She had been his lifeline, the one joy that had lifted him through more than she would ever know.

Yet she had lied to him, had concealed something so profound, so monumental, that he still couldn't quite comprehend the magnitude of it.

Leah was *his.*

He had a child—a daughter who hovered on the brink of womanhood—and Annie hadn't even bothered to tell him.

Questions pounded through him with relentless force, as they had since that moment in the barn.

How had she kept it a secret for so long? What could possibly have compelled her to do such a thing? And if she could withhold something so important, what else was she willing to lie about?

He took a couple of deep breaths to calm himself down. Now wasn't the time to get into this. He had the focus on the present, on all the necessary tasks to make sure they outlasted the storm.

Then maybe he could start digging up the past.

"It should only take me a few minutes to get a fire started in here," he said abruptly without looking at her. "Then I'll go out and take care of the horses."

"I can start a fire," she said, her voice low. "The

horses are worse off than I am, anyway. See to them first.''

He was only too willing to escape the heavy tension in the shack. Accompanied only by the moaning wind, he quickly stabled the tired horses in the small three-sided lean-to a dozen yards from the little cabin, then divided a bale of hay from the small supply he found there.

He knew the firewood inside the cabin wouldn't be enough to make it through the night so he gathered an armload of split logs from the stack outside the lean-to then started back toward the structure.

He had only gone a short distance when his steps faltered. The only light piercing the storm all around came from the small window of the cabin. Inside, he could see Annie moving about, the lantern light gleaming softly off her auburn hair.

The snow being whirled around by the wind softened the scene, gave it a hazy, almost surreal feel, like he was looking into one of those glass globes filled with artificial flakes.

She was so beautiful. When he was a kid he used to think she was like something out of a fairy tale, delicate and fine-boned, with that milky-white skin and her big green eyes.

But there had been stubbornness and strength there, too. Otherwise she never would have survived being married to his brother.

The thought inevitably brought him crashing back to reality. Why had she done it? Why had she taken his child and passed it off as Charlie's?

Leah had said she learned he was her father during an argument between the two of them, so Charlie had obviously known the truth. What could have possibly compelled him to go along with it? It couldn't have been altruism, since he seriously doubted his big brother even knew what the word meant.

In the capricious way of winter storms in the mountains, the wind suddenly subsided for just a moment and that misty wonderland scene disappeared. Instead, he could see the place for what it really was—a broken-down shack in the middle of nowhere.

How appropriate, since everything he thought he knew about Annie, everything he thought she was, had been an illusion, too.

He couldn't stand out here all night unless he wanted to get frostbitten feet. Sooner or later he was going to have to face her. Might as well be sooner. The wind started up again as he pushed his way through the snow and shoved open the door.

She stood near the woodstove stirring something in a battered old pan. When he came in, she looked up and offered a tentative smile that slowly slipped away when he didn't reciprocate.

"I thought you might be hungry," she said in a low, colorless voice. "I couldn't find too many tempting choices here but there was some canned soup in the cupboard. Is minestrone okay?"

His stomach churned at the idea of food but he shrugged as he dumped the armload of wood onto the pile. "Fine."

"It's almost ready if you want to sit down."

He didn't, but he forced himself to remove his hat and coat and hang them on a rusty nail next to hers, then pulled out one of the rickety chairs. While he tested it to make sure it would hold his weight, she ladled the soup into two blue spatterware tin bowls, adding some crackers and a bowl of canned peaches she must have found.

They ate in silence, the tension between them thick and heavy. He didn't trust himself to speak yet so he concentrated instead on the meal. Given his emotional turmoil, the soup tasted about as flavorful to him as that snow out there.

Finally after several long moments, she set her spoon gently to the side of her uneaten helping.

"I hate this," she said, and she sounded on the brink of tears.

"Yeah, well, I'm not too crazy about it either," he growled.

"Say something. Yell at me, ask me questions, anything. Just talk to me. I hate it when you shut me out."

"Me?" The anger he had worked so hard to contain spurted out like sulfur water from Old Faithful and he gave a harsh, humorless laugh. "You hate it when I shut you out? That's rich, Annie. Really rich."

"Joe—"

"You spent more than thirteen damn years shutting me out. Thirteen years!"

"I know," she said quietly. "I'm so sorry."

"I'm afraid 'sorry' doesn't quite cut it, darlin'."

"What do you want me to say, then?"

"How about you give me a rational explanation. The straight truth, for once in your damn life. Why would you do such a thing? What did I ever do to you that made you feel you had to keep her from me?"

Her eyes shimmered with tears in the lantern light and she looked completely miserable. "It wasn't you, it was me. I was scared, Joe. Scared and stupid. You didn't seem to want anything to do with me—you couldn't come down the mountain fast enough after we…after we made love. You barely even looked at me when you left me at the ranch house, barely even spoke.''

She lifted her gaze to him and the deep, remembered hurt there took him aback. ''And then you left town that night, without a word. Not a phone call, not a note, nothing.''

Guilt pricked at him. He *had* left town. Not because of her, though. Because of himself. She had been grieving and heartsick and he had used that in a vain attempt to ease the hunger burning inside him that had grown unbearable.

''Everyone was gone,'' she continued. ''My father, Colt, you. All my life people had been telling me what to do and now I had no one to even turn to for advice. I was a stupid eighteen-year-old girl suddenly responsible for a twenty-thousand-acre cattle ranch.''

She paused. ''In all the craziness after my father's death while I was so busy trying to find my way around the ranch, I didn't even realize I was pregnant until I was almost three months along.''

The day the doctor in Bozeman had confirmed her suspicions had been the best—and worst—day of her life. The news that she was carrying Joe's child had filled her with more joy than she ever believed possible, but it was a bittersweet joy since she had had no one to share it with.

''So why didn't you tell me then?'' he asked.

She tried to read his expression, to figure out what he was thinking, but his features showed nothing. ''I tried. I went to the Broken Spur to talk to your mother and ask if she knew where to find you. She wasn't at the trailer but Charlie was. He took great delight in telling me you were back in town, that you had been for a couple of days."

Her chest ached at the vivid memory, at the hurt and shame she had felt standing on the doorstep of the terrible place where he had survived childhood, begging for any scrap of information about him.

Charlie had smirked at her with such a leering gleam in his eyes. *He knows,* she remembered thinking, and she had been so upset that what had seemed so beautiful there by the lake that day could end up making her feel so tawdry, so sordid.

Joe had been her best friend for as long as she could remember and now it seemed he didn't want to have anything to do with her. He couldn't have made it any more obvious he regretted their brief encounter, and she remembered feeling completely abandoned.

"Before I could find you to tell you I was pregnant, you...your father died."

"I killed him, you mean."

He paused. "Is that why you didn't tell me? You didn't think I deserved to know about my child, now that I was a convicted murderer?"

"No! Absolutely not! That had nothing to do with it."

"So where does Charlie come into all of it?"

Here was where the story got sticky. She thought of the deal she had made with the devil. She couldn't possibly tell him of it. Joe would never understand what she had done and why.

"I didn't see any other choice," she said, which at least was part of the truth.

"Than to marry my brother and pass my child off as his. I see. It makes perfect sense to me."

She knew she deserved his sarcasm but it still stung.

She rose from the table, hands clenched on the splintery edge. "What would you have had me do, Joe? Tell me that. You wouldn't take any of my calls. I went to the county jail three times and you wouldn't even see me.

"I was eighteen and alone and scared to death," she went on quietly. "Worried about you, worried about the baby, worried about myself. I was struggling to run the ranch alone as it was—how could I have coped when I was eight months pregnant? I didn't know how I was going to raise a newborn by myself, too. I needed help and I had no one else to turn to. It sounds so stupid now but I honestly didn't think I had any other choice."

She watched him digest her words, hopeful for the first time in their conversation when she thought she saw a hint of understanding in his eyes but it disappeared quickly, if it was ever even there.

"What about when I was released from prison? Or in the years since I got out? I've seen you nearly every single day for eight years. Don't you think you might have found a chance to mention it?"

How could he when she didn't understand it herself? All along she had planned to tell him when he came back to Ennis. Once Joe had served his sentence and was out of his brother's reach for good, she had planned to put an end to her farce of a marriage.

But for all his crudeness, Charlie wasn't stupid. He must have guessed what was in her mind.

He had always known how much she cared for Joe, ever since that day she'd come knocking on the door at the Broken Spur with her heart raw and exposed for everyone to see.

He had known of her feelings and he had used them as the catalyst for all the choices he forced her to make later.

And while the only thing he wanted from her was the power and wealth she brought to their marriage through the Double C, the knowledge of that bond between her and the half brother he had always despised had eaten away at Charlie like the wind wearing away the sand.

To her vast relief, he had shown no sexual interest in her for the first four years of their marriage—she had insisted from the beginning that she wasn't part of their bargain. But the month before Joe's release, he coldly and without conscience forced her.

"Just making sure what's mine stays mine," he had said. "I'm not giving up the ranch so you can whore for that son-of-a-bitch murdering brother of mine."

After that, after she realized she was pregnant with C.J., she lost whatever spirit she might have had left. Charlie had taken over every aspect of her life, leaving her with nothing of her own—not even her body—and she knew she would never be able to escape him.

At least he had only raped her that once. She wanted to think maybe he was ashamed of himself, but she suspected he realized he'd accomplished what he had set out to do, to break her down completely. After that, he left her alone.

She should have been stronger. She somehow should have found the courage and the will to fight his power over her, despite the cost. But she hadn't, and no matter how fiercely she might wish things had been different, she would always have to live with that.

Nothing she could say would make things right. She could only hope that in time Joe would be able to forgive her.

"I didn't know how to tell you," she said quietly. "And by then I had C.J. to worry about too, so it just seemed better for everyone involved to keep quiet about the truth.''

Not for him. All these years he had watched Leah growing up from afar, envying his brother for his beautiful wife, his beautiful children. Coveting what Charlie had so fiercely it sometimes seemed like a cancer in his soul.

And now to find that a piece of that life had been rightfully his all along was the most bitter of pills.

''I *am* sorry, Joe,'' she went on quietly, sadly. ''I thought I was protecting you and Leah but I can see now that I was wrong. You both had the right to know the truth.''

She rose from the table and took their dishes to the sink. He sat there for several moments, listening to the clatter of dishes as she washed them while he pondered her words and all the twisted events that had led them here.

Fate could be a real bastard sometime. He thought of that summer, how guilt had sent him running but how he had ultimately come back to make things right.

Her memory had haunted him through every single moment of the three months he worked at that ranch in Great Falls and he'd gotten to the point finally where he couldn't deny his feelings for her anymore.

He had somehow found the guts to come back and face her, to see if there was any way they could work out the vast differences between them, but fate had played a cruel trick.

The day he had planned to see her, he ended up in jail for killing his father, forever destroying any happily-ever-after he might have had with Annie.

He couldn't blame all of this on her. If he hadn't taken off, if he had been man enough to face the consequences of his actions, she wouldn't have found herself pregnant, alone and scared.

And if he hadn't been so adamantly determined not to allow her to see him while he was incarcerated—first in the county lockup and then in the state pen—she might have found a way to let him know she was expecting his baby.

He had shut everyone out during those dismal years in prison, especially Annie. When he was first arrested, before he'd pled out and been transferred, it had been self-preservation. He knew he couldn't have survived seeing her so vibrant and alive there amid the dregs of society, knowing she was now forever out of his reach.

He'd longed for her, dreamed of her, though. Even from a distance she had been his salvation, the one shining light in his life.

But then he had learned she married Charlie and he had ruthlessly done his damnedest to exorcise her from his heart.

It obviously hadn't worked.

She finished the last dish then came to stand beside the table, her green eyes troubled and sorrowful. She drew in a deep breath then met his gaze. "Can I ask you something now?"

He had to look away from the impact of those eyes. "What?"

"Why did you leave town after…after that afternoon out there by the lake? I tried to think what I might have done to drive you away and the only thing I could think is that you were ashamed of me, of what we did."

He straightened as guilt swamped him again. "No. Not you, Annie. Never you."

She twisted her hands together. "So why did you take some nowhere job in Great Falls without so much as a phone call? I needed you. As my friend, if nothing else.''

His first instinct urged him to keep quiet—she had lied to him for thirteen years, after all. But then he thought of the girl she had been, how she had completely opened her heart to him the way no one else ever had, and helped heal a broken little boy.

He thought of how sweetly she had given herself to him on the banks of the lake, at how scared she must have been after her father's death, and how he had abandoned her just when she needed him most.

He owed that girl the truth, no matter how painful it was to admit.

''The only person I was ashamed of was myself. I was running from me. I took advantage of you when you were vulnerable and hurting. The day of your father's funeral, for Pete's sake. I should never have kissed you at all that day and I sure as hell shouldn't have made love to you. I didn't want to face you—I *couldn't* face you—and so I ran.''

She was quiet for several moments and the only sound in the cabin was the howling of the wind and the fire's murmur. Finally she spoke. ''You didn't take advantage of me. I made my own choice long before you kissed me.''

He stared at her. ''What?''

''Come on, Joe. You had to know. Everybody else did.''

''Know what?''

''That I loved you.''

Shock rippled through him as he scrambled to figure out how to answer that. Finally he cleared his throat. ''We were friends. Of course you cared about me, just like I cared about you.''

Her laughter was harsh, caustic and completely out

of character for her. "See, there was the whole problem. To you I was always sweet little Annie, your buddy, your pal. You refused to see me as anything else."

He didn't set her straight—what would be the point in confessing he'd had the same feelings for her? Thirteen years and a whole lot of miles had passed since. Everything had changed.

She met his gaze again. "That day of my father's funeral, I knew I had to put away that little girl for the last time and finally grow up. And if I was going to have to become a woman, I was damn well going to do it in your arms."

Stunned, he could only stare at her. He had spent thirteen years ashamed of himself, always considering that afternoon the day had sunk to the lowest point in his life. He had much more to answer for in his actions that day than what had happened with his father three months after.

And now to learn that she had fully intended to give herself to him was almost as astounding as learning what had resulted from that one brief afternoon.

"So where do we go from here?" she asked, when he didn't reply. "What are we going to do about Leah?"

He looked up and frowned when he saw how pale she was. She looked completely hammered.

Little wonder, after the tumultuous day they'd been through. "We don't have to figure everything out tonight. I don't think that storm is going to quit anytime soon so why don't you try to get some sleep? We can discuss all of this in the morning."

She opened her mouth as if to argue, then she nodded.

Long after she finally drifted off, he stayed awake in that splintery, hard-backed chair, revisiting the past and reconsidering the future.

Chapter 14

He awoke cold and aching before dawn after just a few hours of fitful sleep.

The only sound in the cabin now was the wind, down to a muted moan instead of the shrieking fury of earlier. The woodstove no longer popped and buzzed and the cabin lay in frigid darkness.

The fire must have burned itself out like the storm, he realized. With a fervent wish for the comforts of an automatic furnace, he slipped out of the cot to the icy floor, moving slowing and carefully so he didn't awaken Annie, then quietly added a pile of kindling to the few remaining embers.

The kindling caught quickly and it only took a few moments for him to have the blaze again burning brightly.

He hadn't bothered with the lantern and the only light was the red-orange glow from the glass door of the woodstove. Still, it was enough for him to see her sleep-

ing in the narrow bed with just her face sticking out of
the blankets—the fringe of dark eyelashes fanned out
on her cheeks, the little dusting of freckles on her nose,
the soft curve of her mouth.

He rested a hip on the scarred old table and studied
her. Only for a moment, he promised himself. Only because he wouldn't have many more opportunities like
this, just less than two weeks before he would be gone.

She was beautiful, even tousled by sleep and by the
emotionally ragged day they had just been through. She
didn't have the kind of drop-dead sex appeal of some
women. Annie's beauty was softer, gentler.

Like the first frost on the trees in the fall or the pure,
radiant blue of a patch of columbines.

He knew she didn't think she was very strong, but
he recognized her for what she was—a survivor.
Whether she realized it or not, she faced each day with
a quiet kind of courage he couldn't even begin to match.

He had always thought she was the prettiest girl he
knew but part of her appeal had always been her spunk,
that willingness to follow him and Colt into any adventure the older boys might lead.

And her fierce loyalty. There was definitely that. She
had befriended him when most of the other kids at
school sneered at his threadbare clothing and his Shoshone heritage and his drunk bully of a father.

He could remember exactly the day she'd first taken
him under wing, despite the fact that he had been four
years older and twice as big.

She was in kindergarten, he was in third grade. He
had been the oldest boy in his class since he had missed
so much school while his dad moved from job to job
that he couldn't keep up with his own grade and had
been held back a year.

The first day of school had been lousy to begin with. Al had taken the belt to him before the bus came because he'd forgotten to put the cap back on the toothpaste.

His new teacher, Mrs. Latham, had been an old bat, with a white beehive hairdo and cat-eyed glasses and a mouth that looked like it didn't know how to smile. She'd taken an instant dislike to him, maybe because he was so big and stupid or because he was a dirty Indian or because he'd wiggled and squirmed so much on the hard plastic chair, trying to find a position that didn't hurt his raw backside.

Finally she'd told him that since he didn't know how to sit still, he needed to go spend some time with the rest of the babies in the kindergarten class.

He could vividly recall the shame of walking into that classroom, with its little kid desks and its little kid playhouse and its little kid toys.

He could still feel the remembered ache of tears in his throat, tears he refused to surrender to. He was too big to cry, and besides, his daddy taught him early that bawling only made things worse.

Annie had been sitting in a corner playing trucks with a couple of other boys. She'd looked pretty silly in a ruffly pink dress with bows and lace that clashed terribly with her red hair. Without a wife around to guide him, Sam Calhoun probably thought the dress was just the ticket for a little girl's first day of school.

He smiled now. Annie had probably hated it but she would have dressed in tights and a tutu if she thought it might win her dad's approval.

In her spun-sugar dress and pink ribbons hanging every which way in her hair, she watched him come in and sit by himself on the floor then wrap his hands around his knees and bury his head in his arms. In typical Annie fashion, she had ignored all his "back-off" signals and hauled her toys over next to him.

She must have sensed he didn't want her there but, undeterred, she played quietly next to him for a moment. And then she'd done something that still amazed him. She'd reached out, grabbed one of his hands and squeezed it tightly.

"Don't be sad," she said softly in her sing-song little kindergarten voice. "I'll play with you."

That was probably the moment he first fell in love with her.

Joe straightened from the table, angry at himself for letting the thought sneak through his defenses.

Fell. Past tense. He didn't love her anymore. He was still attracted to her, but that's absolutely all there was to it.

Who was he kidding? He blew out a breath. He still loved her. He'd probably never stopped, even though he'd done his best to convince himself otherwise after she married Charlie.

It didn't matter. Nothing had changed. If anything, he was more determined than ever to leave Madison Valley. All his same reasons for leaving still stood. He needed to move on, to find his own place in the world.

And Annie deserved better than another no-account Redhawk who couldn't even walk into town without whispers and stares following right along behind him.

She stirred a little in her sleep just then and the layer of blankets slipped down below her shoulder, revealing the blue-flowered pattern of her thermals.

He paused for just a moment, debating the wisdom of touching her even this casually, then he sighed. It was too cold in here for her to sleep without covers.

Lightly, quietly, he stepped toward the bed and pulled the blankets back into place.

Despite the care he took not to disturb her, her eyes fluttered a few times then opened. The first emotion flickering there was dread and he bit back a curse at his brother who had brought fear into her life.

The alarm faded quickly when she recognized him and her hand slipped from the blankets to rest on his. "Joe? Is everything okay?" Her voice was rough-edged and sexy from sleep.

"Everything's fine," he lied gruffly. "Go back to sleep."

But her eyes remained stubbornly open and a new emotion suddenly flickered in them. Awareness. He watched it kindle to sizzling life just as the fire had and couldn't look away, hypnotized by it like he was by the sultry dance of the flames.

"I was having a dream about you," she said. "About that afternoon by the lake."

Heat shot straight to his groin and he could do nothing but stand there with her hand warm on his and and stare at her. Just what the hell was he supposed to say to that?

"I used to dream about it a lot," she confessed quietly, her green eyes locked with his. "And I would wake up with my face wet with tears, afraid you would never hold me again."

He felt as if his heart had stopped beating. Raw desire hit him so hard he couldn't breathe, couldn't think straight.

Through the quicksilver haze of need he remembered her words of the night before: *If I was going to have to become a woman, I was damn well going to do it in your arms.*

Before he could make his suddenly thick tongue work right to answer her, she sat up in the bed keeping her fingers tightly wrapped around his hand. "Hold me again, Joe," she whispered. "Please."

He tried to fight it, tried to remember all the reasons he couldn't, but he had no defenses against the entreaty in her voice or this hot, urgent need. With a strangled curse he dipped his head.

Her mouth was warm and soft from sleep and she sighed his name when he kissed her. He sank down onto the narrow bed beside her and pulled her into his arms.

She melted against him and wrapped her arms around his neck, holding him tightly to her. The position put them in close contact, chest to chest, and he could feel the soft, unfettered weight of her breasts pressed against him through the weave of her thermal top.

Every movement, every innocent wriggle, aroused him further and he deepened the kiss.

He slipped his tongue between the seam of her lips then groaned when they parted eagerly. The tip of her tongue slid along the side of his and blood roared in his ears.

The way she brushed against him like that was driving him crazy. With some vague intent to stop it, he reached a hand between their bodies and encountered the curve of one breast.

He groaned again, unable to stop himself from savoring her, from caressing her with his thumb and then cupping her through the material of her shirt. She wasn't exactly well-endowed—although personally he thought she was perfect—so her breast fit exactly right in his big hand.

As he touched her, she inhaled a sexy little breath and arched against him, her head sagging back, but still she kept her arms tightly around his neck to maintain the connection of their mouths.

She gave a tiny mewl of protest when he pulled his hand away but it changed in midbreath to a sigh when he slipped his hand underneath her shirt. His body pulsed painfully when he encountered warm, willing skin. She was as soft as thistledown and he couldn't get enough of her.

Wanting—needing—more, he pressed her back against the thin mattress of the cot. He wrenched his mouth away from hers and began to trail kisses along the curve of her jawline, down the slender column of her throat, across the bow of her collarbone.

When his mouth closed over one tight peak, she nearly came off the bed.

Through the haze of thick need, in his head a warning bell began to ring.

He had always kept himself on a tight rein. It was vitally important to him, as important as breathing. He knew some people thought he was cold, hard. Emotionless. But it wasn't anything like that. He just had always had to prove to himself that he could control his mind and his body, that he was different from his father, from Charlie.

But he had never been so turned on as he was right now, never had this wild, urgent kind of need that pounded relentlessly through his body. All his precious control was about to fly right out the window and it scared the hell out of him.

No, he'd take that back. He *had* experienced this rage of desire one other time—when he had taken her innocence on the shores of the Butterfly thirteen years ago.

The thought had the same effect as being thrown naked into the snow.

"Stop. We have to stop. Dammit, Annie. We can't do this."

Her breathing was every bit as ragged as his. "Why not?"

He wanted to bury his head in his hands like he'd done that day in third grade, to do his best to hide away from the world.

He wanted to kiss her again and never, never stop.

He seized on the only excuse he could think of. "Unless you carry something in your saddlebag, we don't have any protection. Look what happened the last time."

She frowned in confusion for a moment, then understanding dawned along with a blush across her cheeks. He wondered why he found that blossoming color so damn appealing.

"I can't get pregnant, if that's what you're worrying about," she mumbled, her blush heating up a notch. "I had complications with C.J. and had to have surgery. And as far as sexual history, I've only been with you and with…with Charlie, and the only…" her voice faltered and she looked away. "The last time with him was eight years ago. If he had given me any kind of…of condition, I think it would have appeared by now."

He gazed at her blushing face in the low light from the woodstove, questions buzzing through his mind. Eight years? What the hell kind of marriage had they had?

He opened his mouth to ask, then shut it with a snap. He had a pretty good idea, but it wasn't his business. And anyway, he wasn't sure he was all too crazy about hearing the answers.

"It's not just that. I'm leaving in two weeks, Annie. Nothing we do here would change that."

He saw the hurt blossoming in her eyes and he hated himself for putting it there but he wouldn't lie to her. He couldn't in good conscience let her think otherwise.

"I know," she said, her voice just a whisper of sound in the still of the cabin.

Was she wrong to want the bittersweet joy of having him like this, knowing he would walk away just as he had done the last time?

No. A resounding, unequivocal no.

She had spent more than thirteen years with only that one memory to keep her warm during the bitter, lonely Montana winters. She wanted more. She wanted to know again the taste of his skin and the strength of his arms and the heat of his touch.

His leaving would be hard enough, though, a worried voice in her head reminded her. Wouldn't this only make her sorrow worse, make her miss him more acutely in the long run?

Maybe, she answered it. But at least she would have this memory to comfort her.

The decision made, she reached a hand out to his chest and splayed it against the chamois fabric of his shirt. "I know you're still leaving. But you're here now. As far as I'm concerned, that's all that matters."

He looked down at her hand and then his gaze met hers. The desire glittering in those black depths like stars in a midnight sky completely took her breath away. "Are you sure, Annie? We can't go back to the way things have been after this."

She didn't want to go back to the way things had been, to the stilted awkwardness that had buzzed between them since he'd come to work for the Double C.

"Dead sure," she replied, with a shadow of a smile.

She watched his throat work as he swallowed hard and then he leaned forward to kiss her. Her pulse pounding loudly in her ears, she settled against his mouth with a sigh. This was what she wanted. This was what she had *always* wanted, since before she was old enough to understand the intricate dance between men and women.

He kissed her fiercely, his mouth demanding, unrelenting, and she returned his kisses with every ounce of emotion she had stored up for most of her life. Their mouths tangled then slid apart then returned together to tangle again.

Before she was completely lost to the haze of desire, she forced one tiny corner of her mind to stay alert, to record every detail—from the unbelievably erotic taste of his mouth to the texture of his skin and the rugged, male scent of him.

His face was rough and in need of a shave but she didn't care. She loved the rasp of stubble against her skin, the wild, untamed look the subtle shadow lent him.

He pressed his fingers to the curve of her collarbone just above the loose neckline of her thermal shirt and his hands were even more rough against her skin, hard and callused from working the ranch. She gloried in it, though, in the thrilling contrast between them.

"Your skin is so soft," he murmured, uncannily echoing her thoughts. "I've always thought so. Touching you is like running my finger over the petals of the season's first wildflowers."

Coming from any other man, she might have laughed at the words, but from Joe—her gruff, decidedly unpoetic Joe—she found them enormously moving.

She smiled softly at him and saw the desire in his dark gaze kick up a level.

"Keep looking at me like that and you're going to get more than you bargained for," he growled.

"I hope so," she murmured. "I really hope so."

He gave a ragged laugh and reached for her again. She wrapped her arms around him tightly, not wanting to ever let go. A low, urgent ache began to pulse inside her with every kiss, with every touch. She arched against him, craving the incredible wonder of his mouth on her again.

A few moments later her wish was granted. He pulled her shirt over her head, baring her to his gaze. She felt a flush crawl up her cheekbones and fought the urge to cross her arms in front of her.

She had always been pretty scrawny and didn't have much in the chest department. He didn't seem to mind, though. At least not judging by the heat flickering in his gaze.

"You're beautiful," he murmured, and pressed his mouth to the slope of one breast in a kiss that seemed almost reverent. She felt a sting behind her eyes, a catch in her throat. She wasn't used to this kind of tenderness—to someone making her feel so delicate and cherished—and she wasn't at all sure how to handle it.

All she knew was that she didn't want him to ever, ever stop.

She twisted her fingers in the silky black of his hair, holding him to her while his mouth skimmed across her skin, while he drew her into his mouth. He licked and tugged, sending heat scorching through her.

She loved the feel of him beneath her fingers and she touched everything within reach—the soft hairs at the nape of his neck, the corded muscles of his shoulders, the strong angle of his jawbone.

His chamois shirt was unbuttoned as if he'd put it on hastily, so it was an easy matter for her to slip it off his shoulders and run her hands down the warm, smooth skin of his strong arms.

He took his shirt off then returned to capture her mouth again and she explored the bounty in front of her, savoring the smooth, rippling muscles of his chest, of his back.

There wasn't an ounce of wasted flesh on him. Every bit was hard, rock-solid from years of working cattle. She wanted all of it.

Amazed at her daring, at this reckless, audacious woman who seemed to have invaded her body, her hands drifted to the waistband of his jeans and began working the row of buttons there.

He froze as her fingers fluttered over him, then he covered her hand with his. ''Annie, be damn sure about this,'' he growled. ''Because I don't know if I'm going to be able to stop.''

The growled admission seemed to have been wrenched from his throat and a vast, aching tenderness welled up inside of her.

He was always so worried about staying in control of himself. He always had been, even when they were kids. Colt used to tease him so much about it. He called him Iron Man Joe and dedicated half his life to trying to make the stoic, serious boy Joe had been lighten up a little.

She could remember only a handful of times where Joe had completely let loose, one time with temper when one of the Broken Spur ranch hands had abused a horse, the other times with complete, uncontrolled laughter at something either she or Colt had done.

He was always so chagrined at himself afterward that he'd let his hard-won self-mastery slip away.

She wondered if she had the power to make it disappear again. And she suddenly wanted fiercely to try.

"I'm positive, Joe." She answered him in a murmur, barely recognizing that low, sultry voice as her own. "I've never been more sure of anything."

Her fingers moved against the hard bulge in his jeans, caressing him through the heavy denim. She was rewarded with a strangled groan. Encouraged, she fumbled to work the buttons free, then wrapped trembling fingers around him.

He didn't protest. He was too busy yanking off the rest of her clothes with frenzied, hurried movements. Soon both of them were naked, heedless of the lingering chill in the small cabin as their bodies generated more than enough flames between them to keep them warm.

He kissed her urgently, his hands and mouth everywhere at once. Her shoulders, her neck, the curve of her breasts. She adored every second of it, loved knowing she hadn't imagined the passion and heat of the first time they made love.

She was so busy savoring his loss of control that she didn't realize her own had disappeared when she wasn't looking until his hand drifted across the swell of her abdomen to tangle in the red curls at the apex of her thighs.

She gasped at the intimate caress. As his clever fingers danced across her, she became aware too late of the pressure building to a fever pitch inside her, of her limbs going loose and pliant.

Suddenly he slipped a finger inside her, to where she

was slick and ready for him, and that was all it took, just that one touch, to send her splintering apart into a thousand, wondrous pieces.

She came back together a few seconds later to find him watching her, his dark eyes stunned and aroused.

Her face went hot as she realized what had happened, how desperately eager she had been for him. "Sorry," she mumbled, hiding her face against his shoulder.

He gave a ragged laugh. "Sorry for what? I think that was just about the sexiest thing I've ever seen."

She could either be embarrassed or she could go with the flow. She decided this was probably her one and only chance to be in his arms like this and she wasn't about to spoil such a gift with something as stupid as self-consciousness.

She pulled free of his shoulder and met his gaze. "Want to see it again?" she asked, her voice hopeful.

He laughed again. "Do you even need to ask?"

He kissed her again, his mouth still smiling, and her heart swelled with love for him, for this tough, scarred man who didn't smile nearly enough and who spent so much time pushing everyone away.

Although she knew he wouldn't welcome the words, she tried to show him how she felt with her body, with her mouth. Their teasing and touching took on a new urgency and when his fingers found her again a few moments later she arched against him, urging him without words to take them both higher.

He entered her slowly, carefully. It was perfect. *He* was perfect. She wrapped her arms tightly around him, not sure if her heart could contain this much emotion or if it would bubble over like a pan left boiling too long on the stove, and she had to bite back the words of love swelling in her throat, words she so wanted to tell him.

With their bodies and mouths entwined, he moved inside her in a steady, powerful rhythm. She arched to meet him, feeling that low, wondrous softening inside her again, that unbearably sweet pressure.

He brought his hands up to curve around her face and the heady contrast between the gentleness there and the demanding force of the rest of his body was more than she could stand.

"Joe," she gasped against his mouth, not sure what she wanted to say other than "Don't stop." *Don't stop, don't stop, don't stop.*

Their gazes locked and her stomach quivered at the raw emotion blazing in his eyes, a wild mesh of feelings she couldn't even begin to guess at. He pushed inside her hard, so hard, and she cried out once then unraveled around him.

With a harsh groan he joined her in a shuddering, powerful explosion. She held him close, their bodies joined in every way possible, as her heart boiled over into tears.

And for a moment—this moment—he was hers.

Chapter 15

They took the High Lonesome trail back down to the ranch in a thick silence broken only by the huffing breaths of the horses pushing through the deep snow.

Several times Joe looked as if he wanted to say something but he always clamped his teeth together and rode on.

She sighed. How could he act as if nothing had happened, as if a few hours ago they hadn't been wrapped in each other's arms so tightly she couldn't tell where she ended and he began?

After they made love, that incredible, cataclysmic encounter that was scored into her heart like a brand, he had held her close without saying anything and she could almost watch his defenses as they clicked back into place.

After just a few moments—far, far too few—he gazed out the window where the sun was beginning to stream in, calmly said the storm seemed to be over, and then he rose and began to dress as casually as if they did this every morning.

They had played this scene before, the first time they made love, right down to his stony, remote expression. She knew the drill—how could she forget?—so she had packed away the pieces of her broken heart and performed her part.

What did she expect? He had spent more than thirteen years pushing her away. Why should today be any different?

No one came out to greet them when at last they rode up to the horse barn. The children were still at Maggie's, she knew, and the rest of the ranch hands were probably out looking for calves that didn't make it through the night.

"I'll take care of the horses," he said gruffly, after they both dismounted.

She studied him, wondering how to bridge the distance he had put between them. The distance he *always* put between them. "Thanks," she finally answered. "I need to get cleaned up and then drive over to the Broken Spur for C.J. and Leah. "

He blew out a breath. "Guess we need to figure out what we're going to do about her."

"I need to talk to her first and try explaining as best I can the choices I made." Some of them, anyway.

He nodded, fingering the leather of Qui's reins. "I have to leave, Annie. For a lot of reasons."

She looked away from him. "I know."

"But I don't want Leah to think I don't want her to be a part of my life. I want to do my best by her."

Everything had become so messy. It would be so difficult trying to explain to her daughter what had prompted her to lie all these years. Most important, she also had to make sure Leah understood that Joe wasn't to blame for any of it.

And what was she going to say to C.J.? He would be so confused when he learned that his favorite uncle was really his sister's father.

Despite all the complications, she couldn't regret that Joe knew the truth. The secret had been a weight she had carried for so long she didn't know how to manage without it. She was weak with relief that she wouldn't have to anymore.

She cleared her throat. "She needs a father, even if it's a long-distance one."

"I was thinking maybe she and C.J. could come stay with me this summer for a couple of weeks. I imagine he's going to be real confused by this and I don't want him to think this is going to change anything between him and me."

She nodded, touched by his sensitivity toward C.J.'s feelings. "We still have more than a week to work this out. We don't have to decide everything right now."

"I know. I just wanted you to know where I stand. You're her mother and she belongs here with you and with her brother but I want to be a part of her life too."

Stay. Stay and be a part of all of our lives. She bit back the words, knowing she had no right to ask them.

"I know that will mean a lot to her," she said softly, then headed toward the house.

Longing only for a shower, she let herself in and climbed the stairs to her bedroom, then turned on the water as hot as she could stand it. For a long time she stood under the spray while it eased the ache from her muscles, wishing it could heal the ache in her heart as easily.

For thirteen years she had managed to convince herself their only other time together had been a mirage, that she had built it up into far more than it actually was.

Being with him again showed her how wrong she was, that it could be every bit as wonderful the second time. She suspected it would be just as earthshaking each and every time.

Not that she would ever know. He had made it abundantly clear they had made a mistake, one that he wouldn't let happen again.

She remained under the spray until the hot water heater ran out and her skin raisined.

Wrapped in the deep blue terry-cloth robe the kids gave her for Christmas and drying her hair with a towel, she opened the door to her bedroom only to freeze, the towel slipping from her hands to puddle at her feet.

Charlie Redhawk sat on her bed, his back against the carved oak headboard that had belonged to her grandmother and his legs stretched out in front of him.

His boots were leaving wet, muddy smears all over her Rolling Star quilt, she noted absurdly.

He gave her a mocking smile. "Trying to pretty yourself up for me? Don't bother. It's a losing battle. Besides, I'm not interested unless you've put a little more weight on that scrawny butt of yours."

Her heart felt as if it would pound out of her chest. She drew a deep breath, hoping to calm this wild scramble of her pulse. "How did you get in here?"

"The door wasn't locked. I figured since you knew I was coming for our little appointment, you must have left it open for me."

Today was the deadline he'd given her to come up with seventy-five thousand dollars. How could she have forgotten? In all the emotional uproar of the last day, his ultimatum had completely slipped her mind.

She tightened the sash on her robe then slipped her hands in the pockets to hide their trembling. "You're trespassing," she said, with as much coolness as she could muster. "I want you to leave."

He gave her that same smirk. "What you want doesn't really matter, now does it, Annie?"

It never had. She had wanted happily-ever-after and had ended up in hell.

Charlie settled back against the headboard and crossed his arms across his chest. "I'm not going anywhere. Not until we finish our little business together."

"We have no business together. Not anymore."

His soft, full mouth tightened. "Seems to me we got about seventy-five thousand in business."

She could feel the nubby fabric of the pocket stretch out with every quiver of her fingers and the knowledge that he could still push just the right buttons with her infuriated her.

Enough was enough. She had had it with men telling her what to do, how she should feel. She was a strong, confident woman and she would not let him do this to her over and over.

She lifted her chin and stared straight into his eyes. "I've thought about it and I'm not giving you any more money, Charlie."

His boots hit the floor with a crash and despite her best efforts, she flinched.

"The hell you're not." His voice turned ugly and mean, the voice of her nightmares.

Strong and confident, she reminded herself even as she fought the urge to flee. *Strong and confident.* "I'm not. Even if I could put my hands on that kind of money, which I can't, I wouldn't give it to you. We're done.''

''It's over when I say it's over.''

''No. It's over now.'' Was that woman with the clear, determined voice really her? Annie wouldn't have believed it if she hadn't heard it herself.

''We're done,'' she repeated. ''Get out of my house, Charlie, and off of my ranch.''

For a moment he seemed nonplused by her defiance. He scowled, looking at her as if a baby kitten had just bitten off a finger, then he shrugged. ''Fine. Up to you. I guess I'll just head on over to the barn and have a little conversation with my baby brother, then. I'm sure he'll be real interested in what I have to say.''

She met his mocking smile with one of her own. ''You're a day too late. He already knows all about Leah.''

He narrowed his eyes. ''You think I'm stupid enough to believe you?''

She might have found this heady new confidence somewhere inside her but that didn't mean she was foolish enough to answer that question honestly. ''Why don't you go ahead and find Joe and ask him yourself?'' she said instead. ''I'm sure he'd be thrilled to see you. He'd probably love the chance to show you again all those clever moves he picked up in prison.''

His face turned a mottled red. Both of them knew Charlie hadn't bested his little brother in a fight since Joe turned eight years old.

He huffed out an angry breath. ''I want my money, you stupid bitch.''

''And I want to barrel race in the national pro rodeo finals. I'm afraid neither one of us is going to get our wish.''

A muscle worked in his jaw and she could see him trying to figure out what had come over his docile, submissive ex-wife. Finally he scratched his cheek and shrugged. "Fine. If that's the way you want to play this, we'll do it the hard way. The money or the boy."

She frowned. "What?"

"You give me the money and I walk away. You don't, and you can kiss your little Charlie Junior good-bye."

She stared at him, an icy chill settling in her stomach. How could she had forgotten the other hold he had over her? "Are you threatening your own son?"

"I'm threatening you. Either you give me the money or I sue for custody of my boy. Wouldn't take much for me to prove you're not fit to raise a dog, let alone my kid."

The laughter took her by surprise. It started low in her stomach, a little hiccup of air at first, then it rumbled up to work its way through her tight throat and exploded out into the room. Before she knew it, she was laughing uproariously, so hard her sides ached and she couldn't seem to catch her breath.

He stared at her like she had slipped completely over the edge. "What the hell's the matter with you? Didn't you hear what I said? I'm gonna sue for custody of that precious little mama's boy of yours. Probably do him good to have a real man in his life."

She drew in a gasping breath trying to still her laughter long enough to speak. "I'm quaking, Charlie. Really quaking." She sputtered again. "Let me get this straight, you really think a judge is going to give you custody of a seven-year-old boy?"

"Sure. Why not? I'm the kid's old man."

"Right. And let's see, what else do you have going

for you? No productive employment for the last thirteen years except sponging off my ranch. A history of alcohol abuse spanning back to junior high school. Assault charges and a jail term hanging over your head. You're regular father-of-the-year material, Charlie.''

She watched his face change, saw his features go rigid with rage, but the blow took her completely by surprise. One minute she was ticking off his less than stellar attributes on her fingers, the next, red-hot fire exploded around her eye.

She swayed backward from the impact and the raw pain.

That one would leave a bruise.

She should have expected the blow and tried one of her many subtle ways of evading it, but the last nineteen months of peace must have made her soft.

Before she could gather her shock-scattered thoughts and step away—or at least relax her muscles to minimize the impact—he hit her again, this time an open-handed slap across her mouth, and she tasted the metallic tang of blood.

He shouted angry curses at her—about how stupid she was, about how she didn't know anything, about how she was going to pay for talking to him like that—and for a moment she was frozen by old patterns of fear and subjugation.

She couldn't think what to do, paralyzed by years of similar scenes. She had learned early that any efforts to protect herself always made things worse. Eventually she had just given up, had quietly surrendered her will.

But not this time.

She wasn't that weak, helpless girl anymore. In the last year she had found strengths in herself she never knew existed and she would be damned if she would ever stand for this again.

Protests swelled inside her throat, then they erupted in violent, savage fury.

"No!" she yelled fiercely before he could strike her again.

The force of her outburst stopped him in his tracks and he stared at her, astonishment in his eyes.

"Touch me again and I'll kill you," she promised in a harsh whisper, and she had never been more serious in her life.

Charlie obviously didn't believe her. "Right," he scoffed, and stepped forward again, his fist already raised for another blow.

Joe heard the shout as he was walking past the ranch house on the way to the foreman's cottage. It was a cry of rage and of pain and he didn't stop to think twice, just raced up the porch steps and burst through the mud-room.

Inside, he heard the sounds of a scuffle and Annie yelling again, chanting "no, no, no" again and again. He took the stairs two at a time and shoved open the door to her bedroom, then paused in the doorway, astounded by the sight before him.

Charlie was backed into a corner by the bed, arms lifted in defense as Annie went after him, using her fists and her feet and her fingernails and any other resource she could find.

She looked like she was more than holding her own and he was tempted to just leave her to it for a while. Heaven knows, Charlie deserved every blow and then some. Besides, it was probably cathartic, in some twisted kind of way, for Annie to finally fight back against the man who had spent years wearing her down.

He would have let her go at it a few more moments, but then Charlie seemed to recover from his shock at what was probably a completely unexpected attack. He pulled his fist back ready to deliver a powerful blow that would have sent her sprawling, but before he could connect, Joe wrapped both arms around Annie and pulled her out of harm's way, still kicking and clawing.

Lost in a haze of adrenaline and raw emotion he was all too familiar with, she would have turned on him as well but he held her close. "It's okay," he murmured in her ear. "It's me."

She stilled instantly except for her quick, hard breathing and a steady trembling as reaction began to set in.

Charlie didn't look any happier to see him than Joe was to find his half brother in Annie's bedroom. He was breathing just as hard as Annie and his cheek was bleeding where she must have scratched him.

He reached a hand up and his expression darkened when he pulled it away and saw the blood. "This is none of your business, little brother," he growled. "It's between me and my wife."

Joe's voice was dangerous, just like the look he sent his brother. "Unless you've gone and got yourself married again in the last few months, you don't have a wife. Not anymore."

To Annie, he said softly. "Can I put you down now?"

She nodded and he set her on her feet. Only then did he get his first look at her face, saw the vivid purple bruise already swelling one eye and the blood trickling from her mouth.

Vicious fury broiled through him at seeing her once more marked by Charlie's violence and for a moment, he couldn't think straight. It was so much like all those other times, first with his mother and then with Annie.

He was filled with the same impotent rage he had felt so often before, knowing he could do nothing to protect either one of them.

"You son of a bitch," he growled. "I warned you what would happen if you ever touched her again."

He grabbed Charlie by the shirt and shoved him against the wall so hard his head hit with a loud crack.

His brother looked back at him with hate in his eyes. "What are you gonna do? Kill me like you did the old man?"

"Try me," he bit out.

"He's not worth it, Joe. Stop."

He glanced at Annie and saw she was trembling wildly now, her arms wrapped tightly around herself.

She was right. As much as he wanted to pound Charlie into tiny little pieces, he knew it wouldn't accomplish a thing except maybe make him feel better.

Violence didn't solve anything—he had spent a lifetime learning that bitter lesson.

He let go of his brother's shirt. "If you want to walk away, get out now."

Charlie swiped at the blood gushing from his cheek. "I want my money," he snarled.

"What money?" Joe asked, at the same time Annie shook her head.

"You're not getting any more," she said. "I meant what I said."

"Then how about I tell loverboy here the real reason you married me?"

"Tell him whatever you want," she said impatiently.

"You really want me to do that? Tell him how you begged me to marry you so the kid he put in your belly didn't have to grow up the bastard of a convicted murderer? How you were so ashamed he'd touched you and you didn't want anybody to know?"

Her face paled. "Get out of my house." She barely spoke in a whisper. "And I suggest you slither out of whatever rock you've been hiding under and get the hell out of Madison Valley. I'm calling the sheriff and I'm sure he's going to be very interested to learn you're back in town, especially when I tell him he can now include violating a restraining order to the laundry list of charges against you."

"You're making a big mistake."

"No. I've made enough mistakes in my life," she answered. "Now I'm finally doing what's right. I want you out of my life and out of my children's lives for good and I will do whatever it takes to make that happen."

Charlie stared at them both for several moments, his face livid, then with a curse, he stalked out the door. "You're going to pay for this," he yelled on his way out.

She winced once when the outside door slammed shut, but then there was silence.

Chapter 16

An awkward silence descended on the room as soon as Charlie slammed out of the house.

The lapels of her robe had come apart during her tussle with him and now she pulled them back into place and tied the sash tightly. That done, she had nothing to do with her fingers so she knotted them tightly together.

"I need to call the sheriff. He doesn't think I'll do it. I have to prove to us both that I will."

Joe nodded his agreement, then listened while she picked up the phone next to her bed and reported that her ex-husband was back in town. Although her voice was calm and steady while she related the information to dispatch, she continued to shake and Joe fought the urge to fold her into his arms and hold her close.

If he did, if he reached for her, he knew he wouldn't be able to let her go.

He focused instead on the practical, the mundane.

"You're bleeding," he said gruffly after she hung up the phone. "Let's get you cleaned up."

"You don't have to do that. I can take care of it."

Ignoring her protests, he led the way into the bathroom and rummaged through the medicine cabinet for something to cleanse the tiny cut at the corner of her mouth. As careful as he tried to be, she still winced when he dabbed a cotton ball soaked in antiseptic to it.

"Sorry," he murmured.

She gave a rueful smile then winced again as the movement pulled at the cut. "It's okay. You didn't do it on purpose." She glanced over his shoulder to study her reflection in the mirrored medicine cabinet. "That's going to be one nasty shiner, isn't it?"

Remembered fury bubbled up inside him and he clenched his teeth together, wishing he'd had more of an opportunity to even the score with his brother.

His gaze shifted from the reflection in the mirror to her and he didn't see any of the chagrin or shame he might have expected. Instead she had her chin lifted and was turning her head this way and that to get a better look at the black eye.

The expression in her face made him think of C.J. when he'd hit the winning home run in a T-ball game last summer. She looked as proud of herself as if she'd just saved the world.

And in a way, she had, he realized. At least her world. For her, the black eye was probably a badge of courage, a reminder that she had finally stood her ground.

He smiled at her, unable to keep the tenderness from filtering through his gaze. "I don't know who was more shocked to find you whaling on him, Charlie or me."

"Me." She gave a small laugh. "I swear, I didn't know I had it in me."

"Where'd you learn to fight like that?"

Her skin blushed under his fingers. "I don't know. I must have looked pretty ridiculous."

"You looked fierce and courageous," he answered, his voice quiet. "I was proud of you."

The tiny bathroom, with its light oak and pale green trim, fell silent again. This time the silence was easy and comfortable.

After several moments, Annie took a deep breath and spoke. "He lied, you know."

"About what?"

"The reason I married him. I wasn't ashamed to be pregnant with your child. I would have been proud for everyone to know Leah was yours—I wanted to shout it from the highest peak in the Madison Range."

The intensity of her voice startled him and his gaze met hers. Her eyes looked huge suddenly and the raw emotion shining in them reached right through his chest and yanked out his heart.

"Annie…" he began, but whatever he meant to say was lost, crushed by his overpowering need to touch her.

She responded immediately, her mouth sweet and welcoming under his, and he forgot all the arguments he'd come up with on the ride down the mountain, about how touching her like this again would be crazy.

Maybe it was, but he didn't care anymore. The only thing that mattered was Annie.

As their mouths twisted together, his body thrummed and seethed, desperate to release all this pent-up energy he had wanted to use up pounding Charlie into pieces.

He wanted to take her hard and fast like he had earlier

in the day. That would have more than done the trick
to quiet the beast prowling through him, but he forced
down the impulse to plunder, to devour.

She didn't need that right now, he sensed instinctively. She'd had more than her share of violence and
now she deserved some softness, some tenderness.

He lifted both hands to cup her face, his thumbs tracing the curve of her cheekbones, and he drew out the
kiss, slowly, leisurely. His mouth danced lightly over
hers again and again.

Her eyes drifted shut and her head sagged as if she
couldn't remember how to work her neck muscles. He
knew just how she felt, as if he were floating on some
barely moving stream with cool water carrying him
along and the sun's warmth soaking through to his
bones.

He kissed the little cut on her mouth, then pressed
his mouth gently to the iridescent bruise forming around
her eye.

Her eyes fluttered open again and met his gaze. She
looked stunned by his caress and very, very aroused.
As he once more returned his mouth to hers she made
a low, erotic sound in her throat that nearly made him
forget he was trying to take things slow and easy.

With their mouths still entangled, he scooped her off
the edge of the tub and carried her through the door into
the bedroom then laid her down gently on her old oak
double bed. She wouldn't let him pull away but held
him tightly to her as he continued his soft assault on
her mouth.

Her room smelled like her, he thought through the
haze of desire wrapped around him. Like apples and
sunshine. Intoxicating and sweet at the same time. Like
Annie.

She was only wearing that terry cloth robe and it was easy for him to untie the sash and pull it free. Underneath she was soft and smelled fresh and clean, like spring.

He shed his own clothes quickly and joined her on the bed. Where their lovemaking earlier had had a fierce urgency he had been helpless against, this time he took her slowly, gently. Her response was the same, though, a sweet eagerness that took his breath away.

Afterward, he laid in her old-fashioned bed and held her close while she drifted off to sleep. He didn't want to let go, ever, and the realization scared the hell out of him.

All of his reasons for keeping his distance from her seemed hollow and worthless when he held her. It didn't seem to matter to her that he was just another no-account Redhawk.

It had never mattered to her, he admitted. He was the one with the inferiority complex, who saw all the differences between them. Who thought she deserved far better than an ex-con with a dark past and not much future.

Annie couldn't have cared less about his past. She had always given her affection to him freely, regardless of how screwed up his life had been.

He thought of her sweet, generous lovemaking and wondered if he'd been a fool, if there was a chance they could break free of the past and find their own future together, the future they might have had if he hadn't gone to prison and she hadn't married Charlie.

A snippet of memory from their conversation suddenly flashed through his brain.

He frowned. ''Why did you marry him?'' he asked suddenly, forgetting she had dozed off.

She blinked awake and stared up at him in confusion. "What?"

He rolled away and sat on the edge of the bed. "You said you didn't marry Charlie to give Leah a name. Why did you marry him, then?"

He had asked her before—hell, he'd asked her a thousand times—but she had always ducked the question. This time she paused as if trying to reach a decision about something, then she looked away from him.

"You," she said simply.

Just that. A single syllable. He waited for her to continue but she didn't. "What are you talking about?" he finally asked.

She sat up as well and wrapped the quilt around her without meeting his gaze. "He came to me after you were arrested and said he heard you threaten to kill your father at Lulu's on the day he died."

"I did." He shrugged. "There's no secret about that. Half the guys in there heard me. I'd had enough of his garbage. I thought things were better, but then I came back to town and found my mother with a broken nose and a cracked rib. I decided I couldn't stand by anymore and do nothing. The only thing Al seemed to understand was a fist so I was going to tell him that if he touched her again, it would be the last time."

She sent him a quick glance then looked down again, her fingers tracing the pattern of the quilt. "Charlie said he thought you were just talking big, that it was the beer talking, really, but he decided to follow you home just in case."

She paused. "He said he reached the house just in time to see your father go down and then you slammed his head against the hearth bricks over and over and over again until he stopped moving. He... He said if I didn't marry him, he would go to his boss at the sheriff's department and tell him everything.''

Disbelief and shock warred within him. "And you believed him?''

"Of course not!'' Her mouth twisted with impatience. "I could never believe you were capable of killing your father deliberately, no matter how much he might have deserved it. I know it was just like you said, an accident. You were fighting and you punched him and he fell backward.''

He thought of all the things she didn't know about what happened that night, things he couldn't tell her. Things that were not his to tell.

"If you weren't buying his story, why go through with the marriage?''

"Because I was young and naive and I was afraid others who didn't know you the way I did would be quick to believe him. You know how Charlie could be. If he wanted to, he could sell popsicles in Siberia. Plus he had his own tight little group of drinking buddies. The sheriff, the other deputies. Even Judge Walters whenever his wife kicked him out of the house. It was your word against his and I knew exactly whose story everyone else would believe. He was a deputy sheriff and you were…you.''

"A troublemaking punk who had already had my share of run-ins with the law.''

She blew out a breath. "Charlie would have done his best to make the whole town think your father's death was premeditated, that you went there fully intending to kill him from the beginning. You would have faced first-degree murder charges. A death sentence. I couldn't let that happen.''

The magnitude of what she had done slowly began

to sink through his shock. She had married Charlie because of him. Everything she went through for all those years—her whole nightmare of a marriage—was his fault.

"I never asked you to be a martyr for me."

His anger took her completely by surprise. She didn't know what she expected—shock, certainly. Amazement, maybe. Whatever she might have anticipated, it wasn't this seething fury radiating from him.

"I know you didn't. And I didn't see it that way."

"Dammit, Annie. I didn't ask for your help. I didn't need it and I wouldn't have wanted it. You gave up your whole damn life to him!"

Her temper spiked along with his. "You were my best friend. *I was pregnant with your baby!* What else was I supposed to do? Let you be sentenced to death, or worse, spend the rest of your life dying by inches in prison for a crime you didn't commit?"

"Yes! If it would have protected you from Charlie and what you went through. Absolutely."

"So it's okay for you to martyr yourself to protect me, but not for me to do whatever I could to help you?"

"I never wanted your help."

"I know," she snapped. "You never wanted anything from anyone. You've always thought you're some kind of damn island, completely isolated from the rest of the world, emotionally self-sufficient."

He stared at her for a moment, then turned away and yanked on the rest of his clothes with abrupt movements.

When he was done, he walked to the doorway but before he walked out of the room, he looked at her one last time. All the fury was gone from his expression, leaving just that cold emptiness she hated so much.

"You suffered years of abuse, Annie," he finally said, his voice low, intense, in contrast to his stony expression. "Do you have any idea how much I hated you for staying with him, for being just like my mother? For letting him hurt you, time after time?"

She had always suspected it. But hearing him say the words, hearing the accusation and the contempt in his voice, was worse than any of Charlie's blows could ever be.

Tears burned behind her eyes but she blinked them back. She wouldn't let him see them. Not now.

He looked away and his chiseled features seemed as bleak and forbidding as the Spanish Peaks. "How am I supposed to feel now, knowing the only reason you put yourself in that hell of a marriage was because of me?"

"I don't know," she whispered.

"Neither do I." He closed his eyes briefly. When he opened them, her heart cracked apart at the desolate sadness there. "And I don't know if I can forgive either one of us."

Without another word, he walked out of the room, closing the door quietly behind him.

The remaining days of Joe's time at the Double C passed in a haze of misery for Annie, as winter grudgingly gave way to spring.

They still worked together, branding calves, riding fence line, preparing the soil for planting as the snow finally began to melt. But through it all, he remained distant and aloof, taking all of his meals in the foreman's cottage and deliberately assigning himself to work with the other hands whenever possible.

Any conversation between them was abrupt, awkward, and she sometimes sensed him watching her out of brooding dark eyes while they worked around the ranch.

But he didn't refer to their final confrontation again and she couldn't bring herself to dredge it all up again.

The night before he was to leave, Annie sat in her office trying again to catch up on paperwork in a futile attempt to keep her mind and hands occupied. As of the next day, she would truly be on her own at the Double C and the weight of that responsibility scared her to death.

She hadn't found a foreman yet, although she had a couple possible candidates coming in later in the week for interviews. Until she found one, the ranch would be short a man during one of the busiest times of the year and she would have to handle everything on her own, from managing the stock to managing the ranch hands.

She had come a long way in the last nineteen months but she had to admit, she was petrified. She gave herself pep talk after pep talk but she still worried that she wouldn't be able to make decisions on her own, that she wouldn't have the authority with the men necessary to run a smooth operation, that she would drive the ranch back into the ground where Charlie had left it.

A sudden movement in the doorway distracted her from her angsting and she looked up to find Leah standing there, wearing the droopy flannel pajamas she loved so much.

"What are you doing still up? It's almost eleven."

"I couldn't sleep. I went to the kitchen to get a drink of water and saw the light on in here."

She probably couldn't sleep because she just as upset as Annie was about Joe's departure in the morning.

At least his coolness hadn't extended to Leah, to her

great relief. She was so pleased to see the two of them begin to forge a new relationship these last two weeks.

As the weather warmed and March's lion weather gave way to a soft, spring lamb, Leah began to spend more time with her father, riding with him after school or just hanging out at with him while he went about his regular chores.

She soaked up his attention like a desert flower after a hard rain and Annie was overjoyed to witness the gradual return of the sweet daughter she used to be. More often than not, C.J. joined them. He seemed to have completely forgiven Joe for leaving.

Annie was uncomfortably aware that both of her children had accepted the reality of Joe's departure with far more grace than their mother. Every time she thought about not seeing him regularly, her chest ached and her stomach trembled.

"Are you okay?" Annie asked Leah now.

Her daughter shrugged. "A little sad about my...about Joe leaving. But it's not like he's dying or anything. Or like I'll never see him again. He said he'll write me and we can talk on the phone all the time and he still wants me and C.J. to go to Wyoming to visit this summer."

She paused. "You know, it's pretty cool the way he includes the brat in everything, so he doesn't feel weird about the way things are now."

Annie smiled at this evidence of Leah's new maturity. A month ago she would have been livid at C.J. butting in to what she probably considered her own time with the father she'd just discovered.

Love washed over her for this beautiful, headstrong child she and Joe had created together and she smiled. "You're a very good big sister to worry about his feelings,'' she said quietly, then on impulse she rose from her desk and pulled her daughter into a hug.

Leah stood stiff and unyielding in her embrace for just a heartbeat, then her arms came around Annie and she returned the hug. Her heart swelled. Maybe they both might make it through this whole teenage thing relatively unscathed after all. She rested her cheek against Leah's shining dark hair. ''I love you, sweetheart.''

''I love you, too,'' Leah responded and Annie felt tears burn behind her eyelids. For a while there, she had been afraid she would never hear those words again. It amazed her that this part of her life could be going so well when the rest of it still seemed like such a mess.

Leah pulled away and cleared her throat, fidgeting with the hem on her pajama top. ''I guess you know I was pretty mad at you for not telling me Joe was my dad.''

''I think I figured that out,'' Annie said wryly.

Leah gave an abashed grin, then looked down at the floor. ''I said some pretty rotten things to you in the last few months. I...I've been meaning to tell you before, I'm sorry. I didn't mean them.''

She hugged her daughter again. ''I know, sweetheart. And I'm sorry I didn't tell you the truth. I know you can't understand this, but I really thought I was doing what was best for everyone involved. I can see now that I was wrong. I'm glad we have no more secrets between us.''

''Me, too.''

''And now you need to get to bed,'' Annie said firmly. ''Come on. I'll tuck you in.''

Although Leah protested she was much too grown-up for something as babyish as being tucked in, Annie could tell she was secretly pleased to be fussed over.

After she left her daughter's room, she walked through the quiet house, double-checking the locks on the doors and the windows. Although Charlie seemed to have taken her warning to heart and hadn't been seen since their altercation in her bedroom, she didn't want to take any chances.

As she checked the last door, the one going off the back porch from the mudroom, she looked through the small window and saw the lights of the foreman's cottage glimmering through the spruce windbreak.

Joe was still awake, probably packing.

The thought stabbed at her sharper than any blade. It was here, the day she had dreaded for almost two months. Tomorrow he would be gone, taking his strength and his decency and his rare, sweet smile with him.

And she would be alone again.

She rubbed at her chest, at the ache there she knew she couldn't ease. For just a moment she was tempted to go to him, to force him not to shut her out like this.

But what good would that accomplish? It couldn't change the fact that he despised her for what she had let Charlie do to her or that he blamed himself for the choices she made.

The click of claws on linoleum alerted her that Dolly was awake and had left her favorite spot by the family room woodstove. The dog brushed past her to the door and began to whine in agitation. When Annie opened the door to let her out, Dolly rushed out, barking.

She squinted into the darkness trying to determine

what had upset the dog so much. At first glance she couldn't see anything out of the ordinary but it only took her a moment to figure out what was wrong.

One of the ranch buildings was on fire.

Chapter 17

Fear clutched at her heart as she saw flames shooting out the roof of the horse barn.

The old, weathered wood of the barn would go up like dry tinder, taking a dozen valuable and well-loved horses along with it.

The Double C would never survive such a blow, and neither would she.

Fueled by panic and adrenaline, she rushed back into the kitchen and fumbled to dial county dispatch, sickly aware that it would take at least twenty minutes for the volunteer fire department to reach the ranch from town.

She couldn't wait that long, she realized as she hung up the phone after reporting the blaze. The animals trapped inside would be dead before the firefighters could reach them.

Her heart pounding, she threw on her boots and raced toward the barn. She stopped only long enough to pound frantically on the door of the double-wide trailer.

When none of the ranch hands answered immediately, she remembered that it was Friday night and the men had been paid that afternoon. They'd probably all gone into town to spend their paychecks at Lulu's.

Joe was still there, at least for one more day. But she would waste valuable time retracing her steps the quarter mile to the foreman's cabin, time she didn't have. Already she could hear the frightened screams of horses above the low crackle of flames consuming wood.

She would just have to handle this on her own while she prayed that Joe would smell the acrid smoke and come to help.

Her breath was coming in sharp, hard gasps by the time she reached the horse barn less than a minute later. She tried to stay calm and assess the scene.

From what she could see, most of the flames were at the front of the barn. She might have a chance of saving some of the animals—and staying alive in the process— if she entered through the door in the back, leading to the corral.

She didn't want to do this.

As she raced along the side of the barn, sweat from more than just the heat of the flames dripped down her back and her stomach roiled with nerves. The fear made her nauseous and she clamped her teeth together against it, angry at herself. She was such a coward. Even now, when animals' lives depended on her, she couldn't get past her own self-doubts.

She was so busy chastising herself that she didn't notice the object in the path until her feet stumbled over it with a hollow clang and the ground rushed up to meet her so hard it knocked the wind out of her.

Gasping, her ribs aching, she lay there for just an instant trying to catch her breath, then saw what had tripped her—a rusted metal two-gallon fuel can. The sharp scent of gasoline still clung to it.

The implications of that gasoline can sent a chill coursing through her. Arson. Someone had deliberately torched her horse barn, had condemned a dozen horses to a gruesome death.

She didn't have to be a crack detective to figure out who might have done such a thing. Charlie Redhawk was the only person who had the motive and the viciousness.

Damn him. Would she never be free of him?

The sheriff had searched the whole county and hadn't been able to find a trace of him. Charlie still had a few friends in the area and several of them claimed he'd taken off to California. They must have been lying for him.

She had been so confident he was gone for good this time, now that he finally realized he had no power over her anymore. There had been no more sinister events on the ranch: no more poisoned animals, no more deliberately cut fences, no more strange photographs.

He must have been biding his time while he plotted this latest, horrible revenge.

Fury exploded in her with more power than any blaze. She would not let him do this, would not let him turn her into a cowering mess again. And she sure as hell was not about to let him destroy her ranch.

With new determination, she climbed over the fence into the corral and ran toward the double doors of the horse barn. They were open, she saw, which seemed odd to her because she knew Joe always checked them at night. It seemed unusual until she saw the crumpled form just inside the first door, head pointed inside the building, out of her view.

Her heart skipped a beat and for a moment she was afraid it might be Joe, that he was hurt somehow.

It wasn't Joe, she saw when she stepped closer. That was Luke Mitchell's black slicker, the one he wore so proudly. She knelt down and shook him. "Luke? Luke, can you hear me?"

He moaned but didn't say anything and she saw his face was black with soot. She realized with shock that he must have gone inside to rescue the horses and been overcome by smoke.

She never would have thought he had it in him to risk his life like this, especially not after that day at the lake.

It didn't matter. He had proved her wrong and now she had to get him out into fresh air. Grabbing his legs, she pitted all her strength against his deadweight and finally managed to drag him through the doorway and out into the muddy corral.

Away from the smoke, he began to gasp and cough. She didn't know the first thing about treating someone with smoke inhalation. Acting only on instinct, she loosened his shirt and untied his bandanna.

The smell of gasoline was strong on his clothing. He must have found the gasoline can Charlie left behind, too, she thought.

A few seconds later he opened his eyes and saw her. He blinked in confusion for a moment and then his eyes widened in panic. "I'm sorry, Miz Annie. Real sorry," he mumbled.

"Shh. Take it easy. Don't try to talk. Just concentrate on breathing."

"Shoulda gone in sooner. I waited too long."

"You shouldn't have gone in at all."

He coughed again, great hacking paroxysms, and she

was torn between staying with him and helping the horses she could now hear screaming above the crackle of the flames.

She didn't know what to do for him but since help was coming soon she decided to do what she could for the horses. "Just lie down and rest. The fire department's on its way and they'll have some oxygen that will set you right before you know it."

"It's all my fault. Your dog. That cow in the lake. All my fault. Didn't mean to hurt anyone."

She stared at him in confusion. What on earth was he talking about? The smoke must have made him delirious. Before she could puzzle it out, she heard a loud cracking inside the burning structure and the horses' screams became even more frantic.

Drawing on the last reserves of courage, she grabbed Luke's bandanna and rushed to the water trough to douse it. "Get on the other side of the fence," she ordered. "I'm going to try to drive the horses out into the corral and I don't want you to get trampled."

His eyes widened even more. "No! You can't go inside there. You can't!"

"I've got to. Those are my horses and I can't sit out here and listen to them die."

Ignoring the rest of his protests, she tied the wet bandanna over her nose and mouth and rushed into the building. The heat seared her lungs, even through the wet bandanna, and she knew she had to work fast.

Most of the flames were still on the front and west walls of the barn and the interior hadn't gone up yet. Still, the smoke was thick and the flames made the place surreal, disorienting.

For a moment she panicked when she couldn't tell where she was, then calm reasserted itself. She knew every inch of the place, could probably muck out all the stalls blindfolded. She could do this.

Forcing herself to stay coolheaded despite the heat, she worked as quickly as she could to unlatch all the stalls.

It probably only took her a few minutes, three tops, but she felt as if she'd been inside the burning structure for hours. She was shaking with exertion and adrenaline as she opened the last stall and shooed the horse toward the corral doors.

Her lungs ached and she felt lightheaded as she followed the horse. Just before she reached the door and safety, she heard another high-pitched scream from inside the barn.

She must have missed one in all the confusion.

Leah's horse, Stardust, she realized in horror. The little paint's stall was the first one from the front of the barn, where the fire was burning more intensely.

Leah loved that horse. Her daughter would be devastated if the little mare burned to death. She had been through so much in the last few months and now she was losing the father she had just found.

She couldn't lose Stardust, too.

Although her lungs now felt as if they were on fire as well, Annie fought her way back through the barn, maneuvering around burning debris to the last stall.

The terrified horse was too frightened to brave the flames even after Annie unlatched her stall and went inside to drive her out. She reared up, hooves flailing, until Annie grabbed her bridle and tugged her back to earth.

''Come on, sweetheart. You can do it,'' she tried to yell, although her voice came out more like a croak.

The journey back through the barn was a nightmare.

The structure was burning in earnest now and she couldn't see, couldn't tell where they were. Finally she found her bearings and pitted all her strength against the horse to lead her toward the door.

Her vision dimming from the lack of oxygen, she knew she wouldn't be able to go much further but she kept up a steady prayer. She had to get out. She had people who loved her, people she loved. Leah, C.J., Joe. Their faces swam behind her vision and she pushed on for them.

They almost made it.

Fifteen feet from safety, a hay bale suddenly erupted right next to them with a loud crackle. Stardust reared again, only this time Annie couldn't move out of the way of her flailing hooves fast enough.

She knew an instant of crushing pain and then the world went black.

Joe sat on the edge of his bed, surveying the boxes containing the fragments of his life.

Not much to show for thirty-four years on the earth. Just a stereo, some clothes and a few pieces of ratty old furniture.

The really sad thing was that even if he had a house full of top-of-the-line electronics equipment and de-signer furniture, it wouldn't mean a thing to him any more than the pitiful display in front of him did. Not when he felt as if his heart was being shredded into tiny pieces.

He didn't want to leave.

He couldn't shake the powerful feeling that he was making the biggest mistake in a life that had been filled with some real doozies.

Annie was the only woman he had ever loved—the

only woman he *would* ever love. He had loved her nearly all his life, even when he told himself he hated her for marrying his brother. She and her kids had become the only real family he had ever known, and he would miss them fiercely.

But every time he thought about what she had been through—the bruises she had tried to hide with sunglasses or makeup and, worse, the bruises he knew would never show—he ached with the knowledge that every blow she took had been because of him.

He couldn't forget it. It haunted his sleep and obsessed every minute of his days. He had worked as Colt's foreman at the Broken Spur through the last several years of her marriage and he knew it was an unhappy one. Most of the time the two of them barely exchanged two words to each other.

Hell, Charlie acted like he wasn't married, with all his carousing. Now Joe understood. A lot of things made a terrible sense. No matter how many times he used to try to convince her to leave, she would always smile sadly and say it wasn't that easy, that there were things he didn't understand.

He didn't then—he *couldn't* understand then. But now he did, with grim clarity.

She had married Charlie in a crazy, misguided effort to protect him and she had stayed for the same reason. For him.

The idea filled him with a strange mixture of awe and guilt and anger. He thought no one else had been hurt by the decisions he made the night of his father's death. He thought it was the right thing to do at the time. The decent thing. The only thing. But now he could see how hideously mistaken he had been. Annie had paid the price for his choices.

Every time he thought about driving away in the morning he would remember how sweetly she responded to him and he would be overwhelmed by all the things he would miss about her—her soft laugh, her compassion, her gentle strength.

Everything.

He rose from the bed abruptly. He'd wasted enough time brooding. The decision had been made and now he had to live with it. He was leaving and it was far too late to change his mind.

And if he was going to take off first thing in the morning, he needed to start loading up his pickup now.

With one last resigned sigh, he stacked a couple of boxes one on top of the other and shouldered open the outside door.

As soon as he walked outside, he knew something was drastically wrong. The smell of smoke was too thick to be coming from his chimney and over the tops of the trees, he could see a strange orange glow.

One of the ranch buildings must be on fire!

He'd been so self-absorbed packing up the paltry pieces of his life that he had been completely oblivious to what was going on outside his own turmoil.

The boxes tumbled to the wooden slats of the porch as he took off running. He reached the horse barn moments later and found a dozen animals careening around the corral in panic and Luke Mitchell sitting propped against the split rail fence, his head in his hands.

"Are all the horses safe?" Joe yelled above the crackle of fire.

Luke looked up, the whites of his eyes looking stark against his soot-blackened face.

"Are the horses safe?" Joe repeated, when the young

ranch hand didn't immediately answer him, just continued gaping at him, his eyes looking shell-shocked.

The kid climbed to his feet slowly and raked his hands through his hair. "She didn't come back out," he said as if he was talking to himself. "This wasn't supposed to happen. She didn't come out."

Dread hit him so hard his knees went weak. "What the hell are you talking about? Who didn't come back out?"

"Annie. Miz Redhawk. She went in after the horses. They all came out but she didn't."

He gave the kid a hard shake. "How long? How long has she been in there?"

"I don't know. Five minutes, maybe more." He grabbed Joe's shirt suddenly. "I didn't mean for anyone to get hurt. You've gotta believe me. I just wanted to show I had what it takes to be a good foreman. It was all Mr. Redhawk's idea."

"Charlie?" He should have known. Dammit, he should have known.

"He…he said if I went in to get the horses myself, I could be the big hero and Miz Redhawk would have to hire me. Just like roping that cow on the ice and nursing her dog back to health after I poisoned her. It was all to show her I could handle the job. But everything went wrong."

"You did this? Set this fire?"

"I didn't know she would get hurt. You've got to believe me. I never wanted to hurt her."

He didn't have time to listen to this. Later he would have time for vengeance but right now he had Annie to worry about.

Joe forced his frozen muscles to move and rushed toward the burning structure, stopping only long enough to whip off his flannel shirt and drench it in water then wrap it around his face.

The heat nearly knocked him over and he couldn't see a thing through the smoke and the flames. He yelled her name but the only answer was the roar of the fire.

His head told him she couldn't possibly still be alive in this inferno. But his heart knew that if she died, he would die right along with her and he knew he had to do everything he could to find her.

Charging through the flames wouldn't get him very far, he knew. While he was trying to figure out what to do, he suddenly remembered a lecture C.J. had given him last fall during his school's Fire Safety Week about what to do if his house ever caught fire.

"Just fall and crawl," C.J. had said proudly, then repeated the chant like a mantra. *Fall and crawl. Fall and crawl.* Scientific law. Hot air rises. The heat and smoke would drift upward, theoretically leaving a safe pocket of air down low.

He dropped to his stomach and dragged himself across the floor, not knowing where to even begin looking for her.

For once in his godforsaken life, fate smiled on him. He had slithered only a dozen feet or so when his hand touched something soft and out of place.

He scrambled up to get a better look through the smoke and flames and his heart nearly stopped when he saw her lying on the ground, crumpled and terribly, terribly still.

He thought for one heart-stopping moment that he was too late, and a howl of denial and grief built up in his throat. Before it could spill out he heard a soft, strangled moan.

She was alive! At least for now.

If he didn't get them both out of there soon, she wouldn't be for long. He scooped her up and, half running, half crouching, hurried for the door. They made it out into the healing air just as the first pumper truck pulled up, lights flashing and sirens screaming.

Chapter 18

Annie watched the scenery between the clinic in Ennis and the Double C pass by in a blur. She was blind to the signs of spring they passed—the new leaves budding on the trees, the random, colorful patches of crocuses emerging from the cold ground, the songbirds flitting around.

None of it mattered. Not when she was so busy trying to hold back her tears.

"Are you all right?" Colt asked suddenly.

She glanced across the width of the truck. "Sure," she said, although it was a lie. She wasn't all right, she was miserable. Joe was gone and she hadn't even had a chance to say goodbye. "Why do you ask?"

"Maybe because you nearly died last night, in case it slipped your memory," Colt said dryly.

"How could it slip my memory when I just spent the night being reminded of it every five minutes?"

Despite all her protests that she was absolutely fine,

Colt's wife Maggie had insisted she stay overnight at the clinic for observation.

"You have a serious case of smoke inhalation and a possible concussion where that horse hit you," Maggie had cautioned. "I'm sorry, Annie, but I can't let you leave."

Since she couldn't quite picture herself trying to wrestle a set of car keys away from a pregnant woman—especially when said pregnant woman was not only her doctor but her good friend—Annie had been stuck all night, being poked and prodded and fussed over.

She wasn't about to endure more from Colt, even if he was doing her the favor of driving her home. "I'm fine," she said. "You can all stop worrying about me now."

"I doubt that," Colt muttered. "You seem to have a knack for getting into more trouble than anyone else I know."

She sniffed. "It wasn't my fault someone decided to burn down my barn."

"No, but it was your fault you decided not to stick around and wait for the firefighters like a normal person would do."

Here we go again. "My horses were going to die. I don't think it was so very foolish to try to save them."

He pursed his mouth but didn't push the matter. "Have you decided whether to press charges against the Mitchell kid?"

She shook her head. She still couldn't believe Luke Mitchell had confessed to anybody who would listen that he not only started the barn fire but poisoned Dolly, drove that cow onto icy Butterfly Lake, and did his best to sabotage the Double C any way he could.

She sighed. "I haven't decided what to do. What's your opinion?"

"It's a no-brainer. You were only a couple heartbeats away from dying in that fire. When I think of what could have happened, my blood runs cold. He needs to be punished."

She didn't answer and Colt sent her a long, searching look across the width of the truck. "You're not seriously thinking about letting him walk, are you?"

"I don't know," she mumbled. The decision to prosecute would have been an easy one—like Colt said, a no-brainer—if not for Charlie's involvement.

But she couldn't shake the feeling that Luke's biggest mistake had been the same one she had made at his age. Listening to the wrong person.

If he hadn't met up with Charlie at Lulu's the night after she told him she wouldn't hire him to replace Joe, he never would have been suckered into the plan in the first place. But Charlie, in typical malicious and manipulative fashion, had managed to convince Luke that the only way to show he could handle the foreman's job was to create situations where he could come out the hero.

Charlie must have been chortling with glee at finding somebody to do his dirty work for him, somebody who would do everything he could to make Annie's life more difficult without Charlie having to lift a finger.

Only trouble was, Luke had bungled every effort. He hadn't been able to rope that heifer after driving her out onto the ice while Annie wasn't looking, he had passed out from smoke inhalation before he could rescue the horses and he'd given Dolly too much of the slug bait Charlie had told him would only make the dog a little sick.

She was angry at him for his naiveté and for the harm he had caused. But how could she blame him? She had been caught up in Charlie's web herself.

Luke had come to his senses in time, though, and now was consumed with remorse. He had even told Sheriff Douglas where Charlie was holed up, in one of the vacation cabins along the Madison.

Charlie was now in custody and it was looking like he would be for a long, long time. For the first time, she truly felt safe. Maybe that's why Annie was more lenient toward Luke.

Or maybe it was because she had a hard time working up enough energy for anger or for retribution or for anything else but this deep, aching sense of loss.

Joe was gone and nothing else seemed to matter.

"Looks like you've got a welcoming committee," Colt said and she realized he had pulled up in front of the ranch house.

Hanging across the posts on the porch was a wide banner with Welcome Home Mom written in fourteen different colors of crayon. Dolly was the welcoming committee Colt referred to. She was waiting on the front porch and when Annie opened the truck door she jumped up and raced over to them, barking and whirling in excitement.

Annie rubbed the little collie's ruff in greeting just as the front door of the house was thrown open with a bang.

"You're home!" C.J. yelled. He jumped the stairs two at a time and threw his arms around her.

Laughing, she hugged him back tightly. "I was only gone overnight, sweetheart."

"I missed you *so much.* Are you gonna be okay?"

It must have been terrifying for him to be awakened

to the wails of sirens especially when she wasn't here to comfort him. She gave him another hug. "I'm fine. I was okay last night but Maggie just wanted to make extra sure."

"Leah says the horses could have died."

"Not just the horses. I said Mom could have died, too."

Annie looked up and found her daughter watching them solemnly from the porch steps.

"Well, I didn't. Everything turned out okay, thank heavens. How's Stardust?"

Leah's face softened. "Still shaken up. Doctor Thacker says the burns on her flanks should heal in a couple of weeks. He gave me some stuff to put on it every day."

"Good. I'm glad that's the worst of it."

Leah came down the stairs and hugged her too. "Thanks for saving her, Mom. I'm glad you're okay."

"Me, too," Annie answered.

"Me, three," C.J. chirped with a grin.

"Count me in, too."

At the deep voice coming from the porch, Annie jerked her head up. Her heart skipped a beat when she found Joe leaning against a post, his arms folded across his chest.

She gaped at him. "You're still here."

He shrugged. "I'm like the proverbial bad penny. You can't get rid of me."

I don't want to. Oh, Joe, I don't want to. "I thought you were leaving this morning."

"I changed my plans a little. Called Waterson and told him what happened. I told him I couldn't take off until I knew you were going to be okay."

Which meant now that he could see she was still alive

and kicking, he would be packing up his truck and heading out.

Her spirits plummeted. At least she would have a chance to say goodbye, although she wasn't entirely sure she wanted it now. Or that she could handle it without breaking down completely.

She forced a smile. "Maggie says I'm good as new."

"I'm glad."

The intensity in his voice and in his dark eyes sent a blush climbing her cheeks.

Colt cleared his throat and she jerked her gaze from Joe's to find him watching them both, an odd, amused look in his blue eyes. "Hey, who wants to show me where the fire was?"

"I do!" C.J. answered.

"Leah? How about you, too?"

"No thanks," she answered.

In his typical nonsubtle way, Colt jerked his head meaningfully toward Annie and Joe and she felt her blush heat even more.

"Come with us," he ordered Leah.

Her daughter must have finally clued in that there were undercurrents here she didn't understand. Her eyes widened as she looked between the two of them. "Uh, sure," she finally said with a smile she hid behind her hand. "See you later, Mom."

As soon as all three of them started toward the horse barn, Annie turned to him. "I...I'm glad I had a chance to see you again before you left. To thank you once again for coming to my rescue."

He shrugged. "Let's just forget it."

"I'm not going to forget it. You saved my life."

"I'm just glad I was able to get there in time."

That wasn't good enough. She wasn't going to let

him get away with clichés and his normal self-deprecating attitude.

She walked up the wooden steps of the porch so they were on level ground—as level as they could be, anyway, when he was almost a foot taller. She drew in a deep breath and met his gaze.

"Tell me the truth, Joe. Why did you do it?"

He frowned at her. "Do what?"

"Go inside that burning barn for me."

"What do you mean, why did I do it? What kind of question is that? Why the hell do you think I did it?"

"Tell me," she asked urgently. It was suddenly vitally important that she know.

He looked at her like the fire had shortwired her brain. "What was I supposed to do? Just stand outside twiddling my thumbs while you burned to death?"

"But what would possibly make you risk your life for mine like that? You could have been killed just as easily as me in there."

He shoved away from the porch post. "This is stupid. What do you want me to say? I couldn't let you die, not if there was something I could do to prevent it."

"That brings the total times you've saved my life to about a dozen, right? Two in the last few months alone, if you add that day at the lake."

He shrugged. "Who's counting?"

"Me. I'm counting."

All the anguish she had gone through these last few weeks—these last thirteen years, for that matter—broiled up inside her and she felt her temper spike right along with it.

She glared at him. "I'm counting," she repeated. "And I want to know why it's so damned okay for you to put your butt on the line for me over and over again, but when you find out I tried to do the same thing for you once, you act as if I committed some unforgivable crime.''

''It's not the same,'' he snapped.

''It's exactly the same! You couldn't stand by and do nothing while I died in that fire. Fine. And I couldn't stand by and see you go to the gas chamber for a crime I knew you didn't commit. Not if I could prevent it.''

He stared at her, stunned by her words, by her logic. He had spent almost two weeks building a hard, stony wall of guilt and anger around his heart and now the first trickle of doubt at his position began to seep through.

''You want to know why I married Charlie?'' she went on. ''Because I love you, you stupid idiot. I have loved you all of my life. I would have done *anything* for you. Even marry a man I hated, if that's what it took to protect you.''

He felt frozen, locked into place by shame as the wall tumbled down around him.

He had been running from her love just as long as she had been offering it, so terrified that accepting it would make him weak, would make him need. In a few words, she had completely humbled him, shown him just how hollow a victory he had won.

He didn't deserve this courageous, beautiful woman who had sacrificed so much for him. Not because of his family or because people thought he had killed his father or because he had spent time in prison.

He didn't deserve her because he hadn't been willing to believe in her. Or in himself.

He knew he didn't deserve her. But dammit, he wasn't going to let that stop him this time.

''There. I've said it,'' she mumbled, when he continued to stand there and stare at her. "Now you can leave." *Go. Please go. Before I make an even bigger fool out of myself.*

"Annie."

She looked up warily.

"I'm not going anywhere."

She blinked at him. "You're...you're not?"

He shook his head.

"What about your new job?"

Waterson would be disappointed but Joe would just have to find a way to make things right with him.

"I've got a job. On a ranch I love." He paused and the silence stretched out between them. "With the woman I love."

For a moment she couldn't breathe, couldn't think straight, as a wild, frantic heat flared through her. He gazed down at her out of those serious dark eyes and the raw emotion in them made her feel as if a thousand butterflies were fluttering through her stomach.

Still, she didn't dare let herself hope. She had hoped too many times before. "What...what did you say?"

"I love you, Annie. I don't want to leave the Double C. I never did. I want to marry you. I want to go to sleep every night with you in my arms and wake up every morning the same way. I want to stay right here and be a father to Leah and to C.J., if you'll have me."

Tears began a long, slow trickle down her cheeks as joy exploded in her heart. "Oh, Joe. Yes. Yes!"

An instant later she was in his arms, right were she had always belonged, and his mouth captured hers. It was a kiss full of healing, a kiss full of redemption.

A kiss overflowing with promise.

They had forever to show each other how wonderful

life could be. The possibilities staggered her and she sagged against him, feeling boneless, weightless.

He guided them both to the old porch swing then sat down and pulled her to his lap. "Annie, before we go any further with this, I have to tell you something."

She drew back, concerned by that solemn look in his dark eyes. "What is it?"

His chest rose and fell against her as he took a deep breath and then his gaze met hers. "I didn't kill my father," he murmured. "I wanted to, but I didn't."

She touched his beautiful, rugged face, to the muscle twitching along his jawline. "I know you didn't. Not on purpose."

"No, you don't understand. I didn't touch him. He was already dead when I walked in the door."

Shocked questions buzzed through her mind, then the answer came to her, sending them all scattering.

"Your mother," she whispered, a statement not a question.

Joe nodded. "She was in the kitchen baking cookies as if nothing had happened while he bled to death."

"Oh Joe. I'm so sorry." She wrapped her arms around him, finally able to give the comfort he had always rejected.

Holding her tightly, he rested his chin on her head. "I think he hit her one too many times and she finally snapped. She didn't remember a thing about it. Nothing. She never did, even up until she died four years ago."

"So you took the blame for her."

"It seemed the right thing to do. I couldn't let her go to jail, not when she had already been through so much. I figured I couldn't protect her from him while he was alive but maybe I could protect her once he was dead."

They were silent for several moments, accompanied only by the rattling of the chains on the porch swing and the beating of their hearts. Finally he kissed her again, so tenderly those tears came sneaking back.

"I love you, Annie. I came back to town all those years ago to tell you that, to see if you might feel the same way. But everything changed after I found my father."

For all of them, she thought. If he hadn't taken the blame for his mother, she never would have married Charlie. But then she wouldn't have had C.J. and wouldn't have discovered how truly strong she could be.

She looked up at the big, hard man she had loved since she was a little girl and her heart overflowed.

It was time to break free of the past, time to move forward and seize the promise life offered them.

And they would do it together.

The knowledge filled her with sweet, healing peace.

* * * * *

V *Silhouette®*

INTIMATE MOMENTS™
and
BEVERLY BARTON
present:

Ready to lay their lives on the line, but unprepared for the power of love

Available in March 2001:
NAVAJO'S WOMAN
(Intimate Moments #1063)
Heroic Joe Ornelas will do anything to shelter the woman he has always loved.

Available in May 2001:
WHITELAW'S WEDDING
(Intimate Moments #1075)
Handsome Hunter Whitelaw is about to fall in love with the pretend wife he only "wed" to protect!

And coming in June 2001, a brand-new, longer-length single title:
THE PROTECTORS:
SWEET CAROLINE'S KEEPER

Sexy David Wolfe longs to claim the woman he has guarded all his life—despite the possible consequences....

Available at your favorite retail outlet.

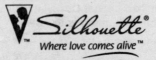

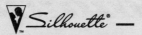

where love comes alive—online...

eHARLEQUIN.com

shop eHarlequin

- ♥ Find all the new Silhouette releases at everyday great discounts.
- ♥ Try before you buy! Read an excerpt from the latest Silhouette novels.
- ♥ Write an online review and share your thoughts with others.

reading room

- ♥ Read our Internet exclusive daily and weekly online serials, or vote in our interactive novel.
- ♥ Talk to other readers about your favorite novels in our Reading Groups.
- ♥ Take our Choose-a-Book quiz to find the series that matches you!

authors' alcove

- ♥ Find out interesting tidbits and details about your favorite authors' lives, interests and writing habits.
- ♥ Ever dreamed of being an author? Enter our Writing Round Robin. The Winning Chapter will be published online! Or review our writing guidelines for submitting your novel.

LINDSAY McKENNA

continues her most popular series with a
brand-new, longer-length book.

And it's the story you've been waiting for....

Morgan's Mercenaries:
Heart of Stone

They had met before. Battled before. And
Captain Maya Stevenson had never again
wanted to lay eyes on Major Dane York—
the man who once tried to destroy
her military career! But on their latest
mission together, Maya discovered that beneath
the fury in Dane's eyes lay a raging passion. Now she
struggled against dangerous desire, as Dane's command
over her seemed greater still. For this time, he laid claim
to her heart....

Only from Lindsay McKenna and Silhouette Books!

"When it comes to action and romance,
nobody does it better than Ms. McKenna."
—*Romantic Times Magazine*

Available in March at your favorite retail outlet.

Silhouette®

Where love comes alive™

#1 *New York Times* bestselling author

NORA ROBERTS

brings you more of the loyal and loving,
tempestuous and tantalizing Stanislaski family.

Coming in February 2001

The Stanislaski Sisters

Natasha and Rachel

Though raised in the Old World traditions of their
family, fiery Natasha Stanislaski and cool, classy
Rachel Stanislaski are ready for a *new* world of love....

*And also available in February 2001 from
Silhouette Special Edition, the newest book in the
heartwarming Stanislaski saga*

CONSIDERING KATE

Natasha and Spencer Kimball's daughter Kate turns her
back on old dreams and returns to her hometown, where
she finds the *man* of her dreams.

Available at your favorite retail outlet.

Where love comes alive™